VAMPIRE CLAUS

ROBERT WINTER

ROBERT RW WINTER
Incurable Romantic

OTHER BOOKS BY ROBERT WINTER

PRIDE AND JOY SERIES
September
Asylum (coming in 2018)

NIGHTS AT MATA HARI SERIES
Every Breath You Take
Lying Eyes

DISCOVER MORE ABOUT THE AUTHOR ONLINE:
Robert Winter
www.robertwinterauthor.com

VAMPIRE CLAUS

ROBERT WINTER

ROBERT RW WINTER

AN ORIGINAL PUBLICATION FROM ROBERT WINTER BOOKS
WWW.ROBERTWINTERAUTHOR.COM

Vampire Claus
© 2017 Robert Winter

Cover Art
© 2017 Dar Albert

Author Photo
© Brad Fowler, Song of Myself Photography

Cover content is for illustrative purposes only and any person depicted on the cover is a model.

First Publication, November 2017
v. 1.0
Print Edition

ISBN-13: 978-0692965160 (Robert Winter Books)
ISBN-10: 0692965165
Printed in the United States of America

DEDICATION

To Andy, again, for all our Christmases –
past, present and future

ONE

ON A COLD winter's night, Taviano scaled what passed in America for an historic building. From its roof, he hurtled to the belfry atop St. Stephen's Catholic church. Rising out of a crouch, he turned slowly to survey the Boston streets below.

A recent snowfall had left rooftops and trees in the park across the road limned in white. Strands of lights wove in and out of metal window guards and dripped from ledges like icicles. Gold tinsel crowns and stars dangled from lampposts. Through windows, Christmas trees glistened.

Moved by the season—and sentimentality, he supposed—Taviano had come to a place he'd never before visited in many decades of wandering. As happened in recent years, though, when Christmas neared he longed for his childhood in Naples. In the nearby town of Quincy, he'd overheard references to Boston's Little Italy. He therefore found himself in the North End to seek out those descended from his erstwhile countrymen.

He listened for a reaction from the passersby some thirty feet below. No one had noticed his body soaring overhead. Not surprising, since the Christmas bustle caught up most of the people crowding the streets. With any luck, he'd be able to relax for one night. He'd like to avoid whatever vampire claimed the area as its hunting ground, and continue to dodge the attention of any humans.

Low temperatures had everyone below on Hanover Street bundled in coats and scarves. His own thin black shirt and trousers—ideal for quick movement but not for passing unseen—would invite comment should someone spot him. A single observer would pose no trouble. He'd simply modify a memory or two and be on his way. But using preternatural gifts meant relaxing his tight control on the demon that shared his body. He hadn't fed it in a few days for lack of a deserving victim. Hunger would make it more difficult to influence.

Far better if he could escape notice in the first place.

From inside St. Stephen's voices rose, singing their devotion. It was "Silent Night" though he'd learned the song with different words. It was barely eight-thirty and he could identify forty-seven adults and children in the nave below. The scent of incense drifted to him, mixed with candle wax, communion wine, and boughs of evergreen.

Christmas customs had greatly changed over the decades. That was something he knew mainly from spying through windows and listening to radio and television programs. Even the rituals of Mass were different than when he'd last been inside a church. Lurking on the outside was as close as he could come. But other traditions had changed only slightly. He imagined the altar draped in white and purple as the priest led the celebration of the Nativity.

Peering down through a glass window of the belfry to see if he was right, he caught his own reflection. Thick black hair lay mussed from the bitter wind, and dark eyes glittered unnaturally like chips of obsidian. His full lips looked mischievous, belying his reserve.

Scruff perpetually darkened his cheeks. He'd been three days without shaving the night he was turned into the creature that stared back at him. Even if he bothered with a razor, the beard returned promptly. He'd heard often when he was alive that he was handsome. Still, symmetrical features and olive skin did not disguise that he was something other than human.

No, even if entering a church were not forbidden, he didn't belong there anymore. No matter how much he missed it.

*   *   *

MIDNIGHT MASS HAD been Taviano's favorite when he was a boy. It was the one night his parents allowed—and expected—him to be awake so late. Once he was old enough to serve as an altar boy, he shared in the faith that his family and community embraced. Calogero, his best friend, teased him about his excitement as the Feast of the Immaculate Conception neared. The feast kicked off the weeks of celebration that led to Christmas itself. Up would go the terra-cotta nativity scene in Taviano's small house, and his mother's baking would begin.

The *Novena* usually found Taviano in the streets with carolers on each of the eight nights prior to Christmas. Or sometimes he would follow the *Zampognari*. In their shepherd costumes, they played bagpipes before shrines and crèches. Finally, the night of nights would arrive. The stories, the magic of Christmas, and the good will in the air wove themselves into a tapestry of happiness.

In the center of that design, the essential core of Taviano's life, was Calogero himself. A year apart in age, and inseparable since they were small children, Taviano and Calogero ran wild in the streets of Naples. As they grew from little boys to young men, Gero never felt the pull of the Church as Taviano did. Still, he was in the first pew on each Christmas Eve that Taviano assisted Father Francesco through Mass. His unruly brown hair and warm almond eyes crinkled at the corner when he smiled up at Taviano holding a massive Bible for the priest.

Calogero Alligheri was everything to him. But even when they fumbled through their first discoveries of each other's bodies, Gero was the one to pull away. "You know this can't go on after we meet girls and get married," he'd whispered to Taviano. "We have to enjoy each other as much as we can but then move forward to our real lives."

The words had broken Taviano's heart though he'd respected their truth. Even if he'd never become a vampire, he couldn't have shared a life with Calogero. Not in Naples in the 1840s. His family, long gone, had been uneasy about his excessive devotion to the Church and to Calogero. With his parents' suspicions confirmed about the latter, they all but abandoned him to the former.

In the end, though, he'd never had to face the moment of giving up Gero for good as one of them embraced adulthood. His death came before he could take his final vows as a priest and before Calogero was to marry Carla Vitale.

Taviano retreated farther into shadow as the choir finished singing and sat in the nave below him. Eyes closed, he focused on the calm breaths of the priest taking his place at the pulpit to begin his homily. Of all the things and people he'd lost, the peace of the Mass and the love of his closest friend were what he missed most. He deserved neither, of course. Years of ceaseless wandering and feeding on the dregs of humanity, always from the darkness, had infected his soul.

After Bronislav put a bloodbeast inside and made Taviano into a vampire, he lectured that humans were cattle. His sire claimed that the bloodbeasts were demons put on Earth to thin the herd. He could still hear Bronislav's hated, rasping voice. *Drink for the pleasure of your demon, and the purer the blood the better. Do not try to enter a home uninvited. No sunlight, no silver, no holy sanctuaries. Conceal the evidence of every kill.*

Taviano had resisted feeding until his demon's gut-wrenching hunger drove him to take his first victim. He remembered sobbing as life faded from the woman Bronislav thrust at him.

He'd considered destroying himself then. Even if the blood-beast permitted it, though, his Catholic instruction left him more afraid of suicide than of a demon. It had taken years to find a balance. He could satiate the creature sharing his body more easily than Bronislav claimed. Days would pass between feedings until its hunger for blood became overwhelming. Taviano didn't need to drain a human either. A few pints sufficed to keep his demon tractable.

And as long as it fed, it had no opinion at all about the choice of victim. Taviano's reluctance to take blood at random evolved into a strict, self-imposed code. For more than one hundred years, he had prowled back alleys and slums, looking for the worst specimens.

When he found a thug or a rapist or even a murderer, he followed to make sure of his crimes. And when he was sure, he stalked the villain, got him alone, and drank.

Sometimes he had to struggle with his demon to stop before the victim died. Sometimes he lost that struggle. If the person lived, Taviano borrowed strange power from his demon to reach into the mind and alter memories. He'd smear the marks left by his fangs with a drop of the thick, clear fluid that filled his veins in place of blood. Bronislav had called it "ichor" and it healed any wound, whether on Taviano or a victim.

Even with those mental chains he forged for himself, he never doubted that he was a monster. He spent his nights seeking the worst parts of a town, the worst of humanity. The bloodbeast never had to be hungry for long because there was so much vileness. He usually avoided people otherwise, in case his demon should succeed in taking control. He stayed in the shadows, as was right for the creature he'd become.

But increasingly he watched through lighted windows as lovers embraced, or haunted a church as he did that night. If he missed the simple joy of a Christmas Eve, well, who was to know?

*　*　*

TAVIANO'S REVERIE BROKE at the sudden prickle over his skin. He stiffened where he crouched, looking slowly around for the threat that alarmed his senses and riled his demon. He narrowed his eyes while the bloodbeast inside his body flexed and roared in his mind.

A sound that no human could have heard drew his eyes right. A lithe woman dropped from the top of the belfry to the rooftop. Her ears flashed with multiple piercings and her short hair was streaked with purple and blue. She appeared to be no more than twenty, though that meant nothing. Taviano was two centuries old but he looked like the twenty-two-year-old man he'd been when his life ended.

Dark eyes glittered at him as the woman flashed her fangs. "You aren't welcome here," she spat. "Move along."

He extended his sense of her, weighing, testing, as she was no doubt doing to him. She wasn't young but he was more powerful if it actually came to a battle. Like any vampire, though, she would fight savagely to protect her territory. Taviano had no desire to wage war where she knew the lay of the land and he was a stranger.

His demon thought differently and tried to claw and rip at the other vampire using Taviano's hands. That mad drive for one bloodbeast to destroy any other, except those it created, was why vampires were solitary beings. They either guarded a territory jealously or, like him, skulked endlessly on the edges of claimed areas.

Bronislav's voice again rasped in his memory: *Observe the customs about territories always.*

With great effort, Taviano maintained mastery over his body and held out an open hand, palm up. "I'm resting as I pass through. I have no intention of claiming this territory." Her stance never varied. Of course not. She expected a trick, or an attack. "*È vero,*" he tried again. "It's true. I don't want to fight you and I'll be away before dawn."

She snarled, "You shouldn't have come in the first place. Boston has been claimed for a century and more. There's no room here for an untethered immortal."

Taviano had to laugh. "Untethered immortal? Is that what they call it now?"

The vampire hissed and launched herself with blinding speed. Her nails raked Taviano's face as she somersaulted over his head to land behind like a cat. The gashes she left burned deeply.

The wound on his face had healed by the time he whirled, but his demon took advantage of Taviano's surprise. His awareness dimmed. The demon made their body move like a shadow. He slipped to the side, pivoted back, and leapt high enough to strike the woman with both feet. She didn't have time to react but shock flashed in her eyes as she collided against the belfry.

The impact would have killed a human; it just stunned her and she dropped to her hands and knees. Taviano, under his demon's sway, wrapped his legs around her waist from behind. His razor-sharp nails pressed upward into her jaw.

Kill her rip her head off feed claim mine.

Taviano battled to regain dominion. He couldn't command his hands or arms but the fight with his demon was on a different plane than the one with the woman. Images had power, he'd learned, and he gritted his teeth. He pictured the bloodbeast as a writhing, spitting serpent that he forced into a cage of steel. It squirmed and hissed at him wordlessly, pulsing with demands for him to surrender and obey. But he would *not* give in.

Pain shot through his hands as the demon fought, burning him with a psychic projection of flame. Desperately, he imagined a heavy lid dropping onto the cage before his demon could slither free. He *felt* the weight of the cover and *tasted* the metal on his tongue as he imbued it with strength.

The cage sealed with a clang and he became aware of the world again, of his hands and agony in them. It seemed the psychic flames caused real damage to his flesh, reddening and blistering his palms and fingers.

Mere moments had passed; the vampire woman still writhed in his grasp. Startled, he realized she was the source of the searing heat. Despite the pain, he croaked hoarsely into her ear, "Last chance. Leave me in peace, and I'll go by tomorrow daybreak. Push this and you will know the final death."

Blood-tinged ichor dripped down her neck where his nails had driven into her skin; he wondered whose blood it was, originally. His demon battered against its cage in his mind, but Taviano unlocked his legs. He lowered his again-smooth hands and stepped away from the vampire.

She glared at him but backed a few steps. The wounds on her neck closed as fast as the blisters on his hands healed.

"Midnight," she spat. "If you aren't out of my territory by then, I'll find you and I won't be alone. Boston is different than other cities. We may not like it but we work together when we must." She backflipped off the balcony into the darkness.

Taviano stayed alert until his demon gradually quieted. Despite the night's vicious struggles—physical and mental—his heartbeat remained steady. He'd learned long ago that, no matter how he ran or exerted himself, its rhythm never varied. It just pumped ichor steadily through his body to simulate life.

With hearing extended to the night, he listened as the vampire ran lightly along a roof and away from him. He sagged in relief; that psychic battle had been far worse than usual. He rested on the rooftop to regroup, trying to calm himself with the sounds of the service that continued below him.

Minutes passed as he listened to the choir and also to his demon. Now that the other vampire had left, it seemed quiescent and bore no anger to him, as far as he could sense. It radiated moderate hunger, though.

Well, fair enough. Surely he could find someone deserving in Boston to placate it. First he wanted to enjoy the Mass a little longer. He lay on his back, relishing the "Ave Maria" from below. His vampire sight picked out the stars that light pollution would obscure to mortal eyes. The air pressure dropped, and he tasted ice in the wind. Another snowfall was on its way.

Maybe it was because his senses were so open that he caught the new sounds. Paper rustled and the smell of peppermint drifted up. A heavy bag slipped to the pavement, followed by a muffled curse: "Shit."

Taviano sat up and craned his head to locate the source. It wasn't coming from Hanover Street, but rather from a lane to the side of the church. He leaned over the roof's edge for a better look and spotted a young man under a streetlight. His blond hair glinted as he struggled to corral a dropped plastic bag while clutching three others.

The bags bulged with loose candy canes and packages in festive wrapping and bows. The young man wore a snug red sweater and red corduroy pants. When he bent over, he displayed a shapely behind and a glimpse of underwear bearing pictures of mistletoe. He had no coat, and Taviano sensed him shiver.

As he watched, the man finished gathering the fallen gifts,

stood straight. He gave a slight grunt as he hoisted the bags. Fully laden, he continued down the dark side street, singing "Jingle Bells" to himself off-key.

The Christmas cheer surrounding the young man was palpable. Perhaps he was heading for a party, given the number of presents. Were he still alive, Taviano could imagine joining him on his walk just as he used to join the men in shepherd costumes in Naples. It was Little Italy, after all. Perhaps there were crèches they could visit together. Taviano smiled at his own foolishness and nearly turned away.

Until he noticed three figures stealthily following the young man.

TWO

TAVIANO WATCHED THE men skulk along the street. From the way they moved, with their eyes fixed on the bags of presents, he thought he knew what they intended. The happiness that exuded from the man in red spoke to memories in Taviano's heart of ancient Christmases. He was suddenly, irrationally, furious at the thought of hoodlums crushing a bit of innocent joy.

Grimly, he reflected that he intended to feed anyway. If he were right about the trio's business, perhaps he'd give his demon what it craved.

He followed noiselessly along the edge of the roof. As expected, one of those in pursuit slipped across the street and ran quietly ahead of the young man. *Just like wolves*, Taviano thought.

The road remained otherwise untraveled, and a lamp overhead was broken. The young man adjusted his bags as his steps echoed on the deserted street. Taviano felt no concern from him and had to shake his head. How naïve he must be, to remain unaware of his peril.

He stepped into a pool of shadows under the broken streetlight and the lead wolf made his move from the front. Spreading his arms wide, he called out, "Hey, merry Christmas, man. Don't know I've seen you 'round here before. What's your name?"

The young man stopped abruptly and Taviano heard his heart accelerate. He answered warily, "Paul." His breath released a small cloud of white into the icy air.

"Nice to meet ya, Paul," the man said, then pulled out a bowie knife that he flipped and caught by the handle. The blade glinted dimly. "Thanks for bringing us our stuff."

Instead of panicking, Paul clutched the handles of the plastic bags firmly. His tenor voice quavered but Taviano heard underlying notes of resolve. "These are for kids in a shelter. It's Christmas. C'mon, man. Don't take away their presents."

"Perrrrrr-fect. You hear that, Joey?" the bandit called. "Your rugrats are gonna get some good shit after all."

A voice from behind made Paul spin. The one apparently called Joey laughed and answered, "Hey, Mike. I wonder if he got one of them Hatchimal things. Laura been askin' for that for months."

Mike called back, "The fuck is a Hatchimal?"

"No clue," Joey answered. "You got one of 'em in those bags, boy?"

Paul turned around again, apparently seeking some way out of his spot. Taviano could taste misery rising from his skin. It mingled with the sour stench of alcohol and marijuana on the three muggers.

Wolves, he'd called them. He snorted. That was far too generous a word for these cretins. They were cowards. Jackals.

The lead jackal—Mike—darted and his knife flashed. Paul hollered and, clutching his shoulder, dropped to his knees as Joey lunged to grab the nearest bag. Neither noticed when Taviano yanked the third bandit off his feet and into the shadows.

When they heard a shriek, abruptly cut off, Joey and Mike both whirled to face the darkness. They crouched low, hands spread to defend themselves.

I'll get back to you in a moment, Joey, Taviano promised as he leapt high in the air. He soared over Joey to land silently behind Mike. The jackal waved his knife in warning moves as he prepared for an attack from the wrong direction. Taviano grabbed his wrist and twisted so the knife fell to the ground. He dragged its owner back into deep shadows before plunging his fangs into Mike's neck. The bloodbeast writhed and thrashed for pleasure as it drank. It hungered to take every drop of blood, but Taviano wrestled for dominance. Perhaps cowed by their earlier battle of wills, it retreated quickly.

Joey was still reacting to the noise of the dropped knife when Taviano tossed aside the stunned Mike. He licked his lips clean and strode out of the darkness. Moving steadily toward Joey, he heard a gasp as Paul spotted him. Taviano continued inexorably across the street.

Joey seemed unable to decide whether to fight or run. His heartbeat raced, fast as a rabbit's when caught in a trap. The jackal looked left and right, apparently shocked to find himself alone and unaided. Trying for an even tone, he rasped out, "Hey, we were jus' having some fun. Teasing the guy, like. Let's all calm down."

Taviano didn't change his pace. He had command, now that the creature had fed. The slightest touch of its power kept Joey from fleeing. His relentless approach continued until he was two feet away, where he stopped and drew himself to his full height. Joey's eyes were glassy with fear and he trembled, like prey that knows when it has met the final predator.

"Fun?" Taviano's voice was rusty from disuse. "If it was just fun, help my friend with the gifts that you made him drop."

"Uh, yeah. Course," Joey said. He sidled around Taviano without ever breaking his gaze, back to where Paul lay sprawled on the sidewalk. He began to gather the mess of presents that had spilled from the bags.

Paul struggled to his feet, keeping one hand pressed to his shoulder and his wide eyes fixed on Taviano. He opened his mouth to speak but Taviano raised a single finger in a gesture for him to wait. Strangely enough, Paul complied.

Joey put the last gift back on top of the pile in the last bag and turned to Taviano. "See? It was nothin'. He ain't hurt bad. Mike gave him a little scratch, like." The bravado in his voice faltered as Taviano came closer. Practically whining, he asked, "Can I, uh, can I go now?" When Taviano reached for him, he started to cry. "Ah, it's Christmas. Please don't—"

A sudden gust eddied the snow around as Taviano used a touch of magic to pull Joey close. His eyes intent on the bandit's, he reached *inside* with his demon's gift and declared, "You will forget what happened here. All you know is that you went out with your friends and you met the worst criminal you can imagine. He said if you ever again even *look* at someone like my friend here, he'll pull out your eyeballs and feed them to you one at a time." The smell of urine reached his nostrils. He spat, "Out of my sight."

Joey ran into the darkness.

"Who...?" Paul choked off what he wanted to say as Taviano turned to face him. "What's happening? Please. Who are you?"

Taviano smiled slightly. "Someone who likes Christmas. Wait here please." He slipped away into the darkness and repeated his instructions to Mike and the other bandit he'd dealt with first. Since he fed from both, with each man he nipped at his finger and smeared a drop of ichor over the puncture marks. It healed them instantly and both jackals scurried away like the low beasts they were.

Taviano returned to their would-be victim, studying him as

he approached. Paul was a handsome young man, probably in his early twenties. His blond hair was overly long and needed a cut. The red sweater, frayed at one sleeve, stretched over a well-shaped chest and broad shoulders. His shoes were quite scuffed, and the fabric of his red pants showed wear. A smell of grease, hamburgers and scorched coffee rose from his clothes, overlaying a delicate personal smell. Taviano inhaled deeply. His senses filtered out the mundane traces of life so he could savor the essence of the man beneath.

Rosemary and lemons and the wind through a grove of olive trees.

He knew he should fix Paul's memories and just go, but he found he was intensely curious. About the bags of presents, and why Paul walked dark streets alone. Why he had no coat, and why he smelled so nice. Since a good hour would vanish anyway, what could it hurt to spend a few minutes talking? It had been a long time since he'd had an actual conversation; he wondered if he still knew how.

Paul kept his blue eyes fixed on Taviano's as he mastered his fear. His heartbeat remained fast but his sweat carried a tinge of relief and, oddly, excitement.

"Thank you," he said fervently as Taviano approached. "I don't know what happened except that you saved my life." He laughed and shook his head. "Wow, that sounded self-important. Okay, you saved the *presents* and you stopped my *ass* from getting kicked." He stuck out the hand not clapped over his shoulder as he said, "I'm Paul. Merry Christmas."

Taviano felt a grin stretch his lips. When had someone last offered him a hand in greeting? Amused, he shook with Paul, whose grip was warm and smooth. Life pulsed strong and steady in the palm against his, and in the fingers wrapped around his cold extremities.

"Yes, I heard you give your name. My name is Taviano."

After a moment, he added awkwardly, "Merry Christmas to you as well."

"Italian, huh?" Paul said as the shake ended. "I figured. You have the look and I hear a little accent. Probably Southern, right? With that black hair and your dark eyes."

Taviano nodded, then belatedly said, "I'm from Naples. Originally."

"Oh, that's cool. My family mostly came from the north of Italy way back. But your name. It's lit *up*! We have three Octavios around the neighborhood that I know of but I don't remember a Taviano before."

"It was unusual even where I come from. My mother picked it from a list of names written in the front of our family Bible."

"Awesome-sauce." Paul blinked a few times and cleared his throat. "So, Taviano, can you tell me what happened here or would you have to kill me? I really don't want that so if it's better that you don't tell me that's great too. Just say so. Dying on Christmas. That would totally suck." He chuckled self-consciously. "Sorry I'm running off at the mouth here. I'm kinda scared and that makes me talk a lot."

Taviano had little interaction with anyone other than his victims. It took him a few moments to decipher what Paul had said, and what he might need. With what he hoped was a reassuring smile, lips together to cover his fangs, he said, "Don't worry, please. I won't hurt you. But it's probably best if we…forget about how we met."

Paul rocked on his heels and exhaled heavily. "That's cool with me. Great. No killing then."

Taviano was relieved he'd made Paul feel better. Like he'd passed a test. The rich scent of fresh blood drifted to his nostrils. "Your shoulder is bleeding. It isn't deep but you should see to that."

Paul frowned as if he'd forgotten, but when he peeled away the covering hand he shuddered. The knife had sliced through his sweater, the cotton T-shirt underneath and, Taviano judged, an eighth-inch of skin. A fair amount of blood coated Paul's palm and shoulder and seeped into the fabrics, but the wound was easily treated. He wouldn't even need stitches.

"Ah shit," Paul muttered. "This is my favorite sweater." He looked blankly at his bloody palm. "That's so gross, man."

His demon sharpened its focus on the blood. Taviano prepared for a battle, but to his surprise, it made no effort to get at Paul. Instead it quieted down and drifted in his belly.

He frowned. Did he put Paul at risk just by standing near? That lack of interest from his bloodbeast was all but unprecedented, and he remained alert for some trick.

Something was different in its reaction, though. It could be as simple as having fed twice that night already. Or... might it have grown to accept his code of sparing innocents while feeding only from the worst wretches? Taviano had been around so few good people in recent decades he'd never had occasion to notice.

Every instinct told him that Paul was just as earnest and innocent as he'd seemed from the rooftop. The unusual pleasure of talking to Paul, combined with his demon's apparent tolerance, heartened Taviano. He granted himself more time to talk, while remaining vigilant against any surprise attack by the bloodbeast.

"Can I take you someplace to attend to your shoulder? Perhaps a nearby pharmacy?"

"I might as well go back to my apartment and clean it there. I've gotta change anyway now." Paul winced as he rotated his shoulder. "It doesn't hurt too bad but that's a lot of blood." He looked at Taviano and asked seriously, "Do you think I should go to a hospital or something? I don't have any insurance but they'd probably still see me at an ER." He muttered, "I hope."

"It isn't necessary," Taviano said confidently. "Put a bandage on it, keep it clean, and I suspect you won't scar."

Paul's eyes widened and he smiled hugely. "I didn't even think about a scar. That would be gangsta! A real war wound, right?"

Taviano had to grin back. "You're remarkably calm for someone who was mugged tonight and cut with a knife."

"No, I got this, bruh. I told myself that I can have ten minutes to scream and freak out later tonight, so I just, like, put it off till then. Believe me, I'll be a fucking mess."

Unlikely. When Taviano altered his memories, he'd take away the mugging with all the rest. He didn't want a dark cloud from the attack to ruin Paul's obvious enjoyment of the season. He should do it soon.

Well, when the conversation runs its course.

Taviano might as well do something useful while they talked. It was almost a shame, since Paul seemed excited about his potential scar. *Ah, but he won't remember the wound anyway.*

"May I?" he asked with a small gesture to Paul's shoulder. "I can stop the bleeding, though you're on your own with mending the sweater."

Paul nodded curiously, and Taviano sliced his sharp thumbnail over his index finger. He smeared a little ichor on the cut, and it began to close. Paul's eyes were like saucers as they turned from the shrinking wound to his healer. Shocking himself, Taviano winked at him. He actually *winked.* "Sorry, Paul, but no scar."

Taviano hadn't stepped back, but neither had Paul. They were almost the same height, though Paul was more slender of build. His big blue eyes had flecks of green and gold around the iris. That close, his heady essence made Taviano's mouth water.

The response puzzled him immensely. It wasn't hunger for

Paul's blood; that much was clear from his demon's apathy. So what was it Taviano wanted to do about that wonderful smell?

Run my fingers through Paul's hair to see if that's where it's coming from. Listen to the sound the silky strands make as they fall back into a glorious mess.

Oh no, that was ridiculous. He hadn't touched a man for any reason but to feed in decades. He was just caught by the novelty of talking to a sweet young man on Christmas Eve. It would end with a missing hour for Paul and a pleasant memory for himself. He opened his mouth to announce it was time to forget everything, but what came out was, "Your eyes are quite beautiful."

Paul blinked and a flush crept up his cheeks as he smiled shyly. "Um, thanks." He looked again at his shoulder, unblemished under its traces of drying blood, and gasped, "Dude! What the actual fuck?" Taviano opened his mouth to answer but Paul waved his hands frantically. "No, wait, don't tell me. That's the deal, right? Don't ask, don't kill."

"What if I promise that you'll forget all this soon, so it doesn't matter if I explain?" It was out before Taviano thought to censor himself. Prior to that evening, he hadn't even acknowledged how much he missed simply talking to someone. The temptation to reveal what he was startled him deeply. Internally, he echoed Paul's crude words. *What the actual fuck am I doing?*

Seeming oblivious to Taviano's panic, Paul asked, "Is that what you said to the asshole? I thought I heard you tell him to forget but I didn't hear it all."

"Yes. The three of them will have nightmares but no actual memories." He worried that would scare Paul, so he hastened to add, "No nightmares for you, I promise. No memories at all." He added a grin to reassure, big enough that it felt strange on his face.

"Oh." The shining gaze dimmed slightly. "Can I be honest?

I'm a little bummed about that."

Taviano frowned. "Really? I would have thought you'd want to put this all behind you as soon as possible."

"Don't get me wrong. I'm kinda scared shitless. But I've never been around a ninja before and it's blowing my mind."

"A ninja?"

"Well, the black clothes. The awesome way you move. You're all muscled up and shit. I just figured…"

This time Taviano's huge smile felt wholly natural. "You worked it out, Paul. I'm a ninja on a special mission for the CIA."

"No shit? An Italian ninja. How does that work?" Paul asked excitedly. "Were you, like, kidnapped to Japan as a child and raised in a secret temple?"

Taviano threw his head back and laughed. It had been sixty-seven years and nine months since he laughed like that. "Oh Paul. You're delightful. Yes, I was taken as a baby to a monastery at the top of Mount Fuji. I had to battle for the respect of the monks."

"Aw, you ruined it, dude." Paul looked dejected and his expressive eyes darted around as his face grew red. "Now I can tell you're making fun of me."

Oh, that wouldn't do. Taviano hadn't meant to hurt his feelings or make him feel bad. *Damn* his ineptitude. Softly, he said, "I'm not making fun of you. I'm playing *with* you. There's a difference."

Paul still wouldn't look at him so Taviano audaciously, unexpectedly, reached out to stroke his cheek. The slight stubble scritched as he curled his finger under Paul's chin and tugged until their eyes met. "Seriously, 'dude,'" he said, working to speak in Paul's modern language. "I think you're, uh, awesome."

Paul smiled at him uncertainly as he assessed whether Taviano was serious. What he saw must have convinced him because his face lit again. He bobbed his head happily. "'Kay 'kay. We're good."

To stand that close and touch recalled long-forgotten delights from Taviano's human life. A simple hug. A kiss. What would Paul feel like, enfolded in his arms? Would he be warm? His brazen hand, still on Paul's chin, trembled slightly. Their eyes locked together, and Paul's lips slackened. He tilted his head forward minutely. An invitation, and all Taviano had to do was lean in—

A siren roared by on Hanover Street, shattering the stillness. Shaking his head, Taviano dropped his hand and stepped back. He reached for any topic that would cover his near-blunder but keep the conversation going. In a voice unsteady to his own ears, he blurted, "Tell me about the presents."

"Oh! Right." Paul attempted to adjust his pants discreetly. Failed. Saw that he'd failed and blushed, then stammered, "Yeah, so there's this shelter for LGBTQ kids a couple of blocks over. I've volunteered there for a few months. Most of them are great teenagers who got dealt a shitty hand. They're on the lists for all those Christmas gift programs, you know? But somehow the queer kids didn't get picked when Joe and Brenda Suburb did their guilt-ridden thing."

Taviano tried to apply the snatches of talk and programs he'd overheard through the years. He furrowed his brow. "I think I understood every other word of that."

Paul rolled his eyes. "I guess the ninja monastery didn't have TV. Anyway, these kids were gonna get shafted come Christmas morning, like, by the biggest dick without lube."

"That's...painfully descriptive," Taviano chuckled.

"Whatever. Prude," Paul muttered with a grin as he tried to gather his bags of gifts. When he struggled, Taviano stepped over and took the three largest bags effortlessly while Paul hoisted the last one. He began to walk back in the direction he'd come from, and after a pause, Taviano followed him up the street. *Just a little longer…*

"Anyway," Paul continued, "I started a fund at the diner where I work. I put signs on the counter and set out jars. I guilted every motherfucker who walked through the door until I got at least a dollar out of 'em. Then I started making my way through the shelter's list of residents. I couldn't get everything they wanted—even homeless kids can be greedy, you know?—but I made sure every child will have at least one cool present to open on Christmas morning."

"That's remarkable," Taviano said admiringly. Given the state of his clothes, it seemed likely that Paul owned little himself. Despite that, he had the generosity of heart to worry about children with even less. Decades of taking blood from the darkest specimens of humanity had clouded Taviano's perceptions. He'd nearly forgotten that there were good people in the world as well. People like Paul.

"Did it take long to gather the funds?"

"Oh, not really. I only started raising money after Thanksgiving. I'd go on shopping trips when I could hitch a ride with a cousin who has a car. Storing all the shit was a problem, though, because my place is fucking tiny. Like, two hundred square feet small."

"Hmm. That sounds gigantic after the cell I lived in at my monastery."

Paul shot a glance back over his shoulder. "Ah man, we're not gonna play who's had it worse. You ended up with ninja skills and super powers. I'm a short order cook. I win."

Taviano laughed. "Let's call it a draw." Paul flashed him a grin and it was the sweetest thing Taviano had seen in a very long time. He wanted to see it again. Besides, he might actually have started to remember how to talk normally. How to banter.

Or at least, not act like a monstrous recluse who ate everyone he met.

"Where are we going now?" he asked. "Your tiny cell?"

"Yeah. My place." Paul's ears turned red. "I need to change or I'll scare the shit out of the kids at the shelter."

A new scent surrounded Paul. It took a moment for Taviano to process and isolate it from the essence of rosemary and lemons.

It was pheromones. Arousal. The idea of bringing Taviano to his apartment excited Paul.

For that matter, it excited Taviano.

THREE

TRAILING BEHIND PAUL, Taviano began to wonder why he was there. Serving as protector and porter to a would-be Christmas elf… It seemed ridiculous. Yet Paul radiated happiness as he told random stories about diner patrons he'd asked for money. Taviano hadn't experienced that in a very long time.

There were certainly worse ways to spend a Christmas Eve. As his demon remained calm and apparently disinterested, Paul seemed to be in no danger. Taviano found himself smiling and loose-limbed, and so he chose to see how matters progressed.

They walked along Charters Street to an increasingly shabby neighborhood. Paul steered over and around snow piled into mounds of ice mixed with dirt. The bags of gifts were light in Taviano's arms as he focused on the luminous man. Chattering and gossiping, Paul led them away from the lights and noise of busy Boston streets. Eventually they turned down a dark road littered with empty cans and trash bags.

Paul stopped at a heavy metal door situated in a brick wall. The setting was barren; Taviano couldn't imagine someone living there. He wondered amusedly if Paul actually planned to mug *him*.

Paul pulled a set of keys out of his pocket and stuck one into the big lock set in the metal door. From the dents and scuffs around the handle, it was obvious more than one person had tried to break in. Taviano couldn't fathom why.

When Paul finally pulled the heavy door open and entered the building, Taviano was moderately curious. Would the magic that protected a home from his kind prevent him from following? He stepped gingerly over the threshold.

No, that was easy. Apparently many people traveled in and out of the common spaces of the building. No one could claim it as a personal sanctuary.

Paul's apartment would likely be the barrier, though.

They climbed three flights of stairs to a door marked with a "4" in spray paint. Paul fumbled with his keys before unlocking the deadbolt and handle. He pushed the door open and went through, calling behind him, "Put the bags anywhere."

Taviano stopped in the hallway. His toes brushed rubber molding that separated the concrete floor from the linoleum of Paul's apartment. To his vampire eyes, it appeared as if a thick pane of glass covered the doorway. From years of testing when he was newly dead, he knew he lacked the power to force his way through the barrier.

Bronislav had warned him about the barrier magic and the many other prohibitions. After a handful of years, though, he'd dared to rebel and try to enter a few homes uninvited. Always he failed. Once, he even let the bloodbeast out entirely to see if it could break through. That had proved to be a costly mistake, and still he failed to get inside by force.

Taviano said, "I'll wait out here."

Paul paused in the middle of yanking off his damaged sweater, his head and arms all in a tangle. "Dude. Please come in."

And like that, the barrier dissolved. Whatever its source, simple words of uncoerced invitation were enough to send it back to the ether from which it sprang.

The casualness of Paul in welcoming a predator, a killer, into his home warmed Taviano's heart. Paul had seen a fraction of what he could do. Even if he didn't guess the extent of his risk, he had to know at some level that Taviano was dangerous. Yet he didn't hesitate to open his home. *So naïve. So sweet.*

Taviano grinned as he stepped over the threshold and tested out the jargon he collected from Paul. *Whatever, dude.*

The apartment was indeed small, a studio with exposed brick walls and two white-cased windows. Through them he could see a fire escape and then, across the street, a tiled roof. The latch on the right window had broken. *Foolish man*, he thought as he watched Paul hop on one foot to take off a boot. *Let a monster in the front door. Invite a robber through the window. How are you still alive?*

He surveyed the rest of Paul's home. An open door revealed a small bathroom. The opposite wall contained a two-burner stove, a sink, and a half-sized refrigerator. A wooden café table sat with two mismatched chairs. A futon couch along another wall likely served as Paul's bed.

Next to it was a milk crate on which sat a tiny Christmas tree, wrapped in blue and yellow lights. A few small ornaments dangled from its boughs, though no presents rested underneath. That struck Taviano as sad, given the work Paul had gone through to gather gifts for the homeless youths.

A distinct combination of smells tickled his nose from the area of the futon. Besides Paul's unique scent there were echoes of other men. Different colognes or bathing products. Latex, foil, something oily, and then…

Taviano turned away as he identified traces of semen. The turmoil in his chest that the evidence of Paul's life produced disturbed him. If he could blush, he would.

Paul finished with his boots and socks and tugged off his

bloodied T-shirt. Tossing the garments in a heap on the floor, he strode to the sink. Dressed only in low-slung corduroys, he turned on the faucet and began to scrub away dried blood on his shoulder and palm.

Taviano took in the sight of lean muscle, flexing under pale skin as Paul washed. That skin reminded him of cream. A tattoo of a tree adorned Paul's back. Its delicately drawn branches spread to his shoulders. The twisted and sturdy trunk disappeared into the mistletoe-themed boxers resting low on his hips. One side of the tree showed a splintered stump, as if someone had wrenched off a branch.

Although curious about the imagery, Taviano wondered more how that inked skin would feel under his lips. Then he wondered *why* he wondered. His demon's hunger for blood drove him for such long years. He'd all but forgotten what it was like to hunger for touch.

Year after year, he hunted with a singular purpose, among people useful to him only as food. Yet he found himself imagining what it would be like to draw Paul against his body. The warmth would be delicious. Soothing. It reminded Taviano of the difference between *appetite* and *attraction*. He found the thought both sobering and exciting.

Twice, many decades ago, and before he began to hunt exclusively among villains, he'd given in to curiosity. He'd caressed a willing man with his sensitive fingertips, and even allowed him to stroke Taviano with lust. Both times, the sensation was too intense to be pleasurable. It had been like dragging woolen cloth over a sunburn.

Neither encounter had smelled like Paul, though. Would the taste of his skin be as unique as his scent? Would his body be warm and welcoming? Why should just one man out of the multitudes he'd encountered draw him so profoundly and calm his demon? If he touched Paul once, Taviano wasn't sure he'd want to stop.

Paul turned from the sink to grab a hand towel and caught Taviano staring at him. Another tattoo, of a sun rising above a mountain range, sprawled down his left pectoral. He stilled but made no effort to cover his hair-dusted and spare torso.

Instead he stood silently as Taviano studied him. His eyes caressed the alabaster planes of Paul's chest, the sinewy shoulders and elegantly tapered arms. He admired the tight skin at Paul's stomach, the tracing of fine hair that disappeared down into his boxers. Paul began to breathe more heavily under the scrutiny and his pants tented outward. Taviano smelled arousal and it echoed in his own belly.

Finally Paul swiped the cloth against his shoulder and dried his hands while holding Taviano's eyes. He licked his lips and flushed. In a slightly hoarse voice, he asked, "Did I get it all?"

As if drawn by a magnet, Taviano stepped closer, hearing Paul's heart beat faster at his approach. His body glistened in the dim light of the room. Taviano sensed no fear as he took another step and peered at Paul's shoulder. He brushed trembling fingertips over clean white skin and murmured, "It looks perfect."

Thankfully his face couldn't blush and his heart couldn't pound; he was sure he'd be a sight to behold otherwise. The desire to touch, to stroke, was difficult to hide, from Paul and from himself. Paul stood mere inches away. His coursing, rich blood generated warmth that called to Taviano. For once, it had nothing to do with his demon's clamor for food.

The bloodbeast remained strangely quiet, drifting in his belly and mind, but asleep. With that awareness, Taviano finally had to admit that the yearning he felt was entirely his own.

Paul's lips parted and his nostrils flared as he met Taviano's gaze. His pupils were wide and black. Heat rose from his groin where he was hard and Taviano smelled precome leaking.

Just touch him. It isn't like Naples. No one will punish us.

Yet he couldn't move into the caress he wanted desperately.

Perhaps Paul saw the struggle in his eyes, or was simply less afraid. "You are seriously beautiful," he whispered. He moved closer and tilted his head slightly. "Can I kiss you?" Taviano swallowed, then nodded sharply. Paul slid one hand up his waist and raised the other to curl around his neck. He gently tugged Taviano forward until their lips met.

The sweetness and warmth of Paul's mouth threatened to undo him. He felt every minute crease in the cold-chapped lips, but the movement against his own was light and careful. He tensed for discomfort from the stroke of Paul's hand over his skin or the press of his mouth. It never came. The gentleness with which Paul embraced him was a balm. Fingers combed through the hair at the base of Taviano's neck before sliding to grip the back of his skull.

The boy Taviano had been still fretted in his memories. All the teachings of his youth had warned that his desires were shameful. His angry father had beaten that lesson into his back. Then, ever since he'd turned, his humanity had served only his demon. His body was merely a vessel to give it agency. His limbs had power in order to subdue prey. He hunted, cornered, grasped, pierced, and drank to keep it fed. He was a devil; if he ever yearned for the things he'd discovered with Calogero, their loss was necessary. It was only proper that he suffer.

Paul's hands in his hair, though… The intimacy sent a shiver through Taviano. He'd missed so much over the long years. The world had changed, and what it forbade in his youth common in the current era.

Common, perhaps, but still special. Drawing strength from Paul's touch, Taviano resolved to fight his doubts and kissed back with growing passion. When Paul sighed with pleasure, his breath tasted of peppermint. Taviano smiled; Paul had licked one of the candy canes he bought for the shelter.

I'm actually doing this, he thought with wonder. *Touching instead of taking. Kissing instead of drinking.*

Doubt faded away. The feeling that replaced it, that bubbled through his chest, had been absent for so long he almost didn't recognize it. He was happy.

Stirred by the unfamiliar emotion, he wrapped his arms securely around Paul. He was careful of the fragile body he held. Paul's erection pressed against his hip, and Taviano permitted himself to strive for more connection.

A memory of explorations with Calogero occurred to him. He darted a lick across the seam of Paul's mouth. Paul opened to let him inside, and a thrill ran through him all over again. Their tongues met and danced and explored. Paul was eager and passionate; the more Taviano responded, the higher he drove the embrace.

Their bodies moved together. The rustle of Taviano's black shirt against bare skin sounded, to his vampire ears, like raven wings. Paul's hard shaft pressing against him brought back other things that had been similarly forbidden. Maybe, he mused, they could go even further than kissing.

He splayed a hand on Paul's bare back and traced lightly over the tree formed of ink, its texture guiding his sensitive fingers. Paul arched at the exploration; gooseflesh broke out under Taviano's touch. Nipples hardened to firm points against Taviano's chest as Paul deepened their kiss in response. He slid his tongue between Taviano's lower gum and the teeth there, then pressed it flat against the roof of his mouth. He glided to the right, reaching the eyetooth–

Paul jerked his head away and held a hand against his mouth.

The saucer eyes were back, and his heart became a jackhammer. "You aren't a ninja, are you?" he demanded on a shaky exhale.

Oh no, please, not yet. Taviano should have known that discovery was inevitable, but still he wasn't ready. The simple pleasure of conversing with a man, of exploring an attraction, of *kissing...* He had no idea how much he'd longed for all that until Paul gave it to him, and then took it away. He wanted to weep suddenly, but instead he steeled against regret. What he desired was for the humans. He had no business there, no right to sully Paul with his devilish presence.

Paul would scream or run, no doubt. He dropped his hands, preparing to let the night become no more than a fond recollection to keep him company in years to come. *It's time to deal with Paul's memories anyway,* he thought wretchedly, establishing as much distance as he could.

Yet before he could pull away, Paul clutched at his waist as if to keep *him* from bolting. Taviano still felt Paul's hard member against his thigh. Whether from naiveté or the thrill of danger, Paul clung to the fiend he'd let into his home.

A small tingle of hope lit up Taviano's chest. Perhaps it didn't have to end so quickly after all? He quirked an eyebrow and tried on a grin. "No. Not a ninja." *Tell him. Let him choose.* Every part of Taviano's brain screamed that it was a terrible idea, but he asked, "Do you want to know?"

Paul swallowed hard but nodded. Made brave by the hand around his waist, Taviano leaned closer. He brushed his lips back and forth against Paul's cheek and readied to say what he'd never before spoken aloud. Paul's heart thundered in his chest. The rush of blood made his long, hard cock pulse between them.

Taviano whispered a word into his ear. "Vampire."

FOUR

PAUL TREMBLED IN Taviano's arms but made no effort to disengage. "Well, that makes more sense than ninja," he finally said, then "I don't know what to think about that."

Leaning back enough to meet his eyes, Taviano found belief and acceptance coupled with nothing more than slight shock. Paul wasn't afraid of him, just stunned.

The trust staggered him.

"You don't have to think anything about it, Paul. It just is." Taviano brushed a thumb over Paul's lower lip. "I'm glad you believe me, but, *why* do you?"

Paul licked the thumb against his mouth and clutched Taviano more surely. "Honestly? I'm not sure. But what I saw you do, and then the thing with your blood on my cut, and your fangs…" He choked off and trembled violently in Taviano's arms though he never let go. "Holy fuck. You're a *vampire!*"

Concern shot through Taviano and woke his demon, but it realized the lack of danger and quieted again with no fuss. Nevertheless, Taviano remained on guard against it as he swore, "I promise. I won't hurt you."

Paul rested his head against Taviano's shoulder, and that was response enough. The quivering in his body eased and quieted until, amazingly, he gave a small chuckle. "My *nonna* says I should ask more questions before I bring someone home."

"You talk to your grandmother about your, uh, men?" Taviano heard the scandalized edge to his own question.

Paul raised his head long enough to smirk. "Not the deets. Duh. She's supercool, except she thinks I'm not careful enough."

"She's right, of course."

"Oh, not you too." Paul smiled broadly and pushed at Taviano's shoulder. "'Sides, I'm all talk. I hook up once, maybe twice a month, and we always use rubbers."

A peculiar feeling stirred in Taviano's chest and made him clench his jaw. A sudden image flashed in his head, of tracking the most recent man whose seed spattered the futon. He saw himself plunge fangs into the cretin's neck, for touching Paul. The satisfaction that vision produced had nothing to do with feeding.

Vaguely, his demon throbbed with amusement. When Taviano realized it was *laughing* at him he became flustered. To cover, he said again, "I wouldn't hurt you, Paul. Soon I'll help you forget and it can all be over."

The shine in Paul's face dimmed and he asked in a low voice, "Will you...? Can I at least remember it as a hot dream? I mean, how many people get it on with a vampire?"

Taviano smiled. "Yes, I can do that for you." *But it doesn't have to be right away, does it?* Tilting Paul's chin up, he could look into those lovely blue eyes as he asked, "You know what I am now. Would you let me kiss you anyway?"

Paul didn't even answer, but lunged for Taviano's lips like he starved for the contact. If there had been passion before, this time there was fire. His tongue was agile and coaxing, drawing Taviano onward with increasingly desperate moans. He tugged at his lower lip with teeth, and used the tip of his tongue to probe gently at Taviano's fangs. Obviously fascinated by the needle-sharp points, he licked up each deadly spike.

The intimacy of that raspy touch over first the left fang, then the right, made Taviano stiffen with alarm. Then the sheer daring of it broke through his reserve. With a growl deep in his throat, he pressed Paul against a wall.

As Paul's words had let Taviano enter his apartment, so his grip called the vampire to enjoy his body. And enjoy it he did. He explored freely with his hands, roaming up and down Paul's arms and he plundered Paul's mouth. He caged Paul with his body, conscious of his own strength and the fragility of the man in his arms.

Finally Paul broke the embrace and sagged, gasping, "Oh man. You got game."

"What does that mean?"

Paul pressed his forehead to Taviano's. "It means you kiss great. Like, seriously great." He lowered his cheek to rest against Taviano's chest and rubbed like a cat. "I get it now," he murmured. "Your skin is cold but you're full of heat."

"I'm sorry about my cold skin," Taviano said, trying to step away.

Paul gripped him more tightly. "Don't let go. It's different, not bad. You hold me like you mean it." He ran his palm across Taviano's back. "I should have a shitload of questions but I'm just wondering... Do you have to work out to keep all this muscle?"

He laughed gently. "No. It's one of the perquisites of the deal. My body operates at peak efficiency, even if I never go near a gymnasium."

Paul met his eyes again, all earnest and curious and guileless. "But like, blood drinking and undead and all that shit? It's really like that?"

The expression on his face moved Taviano and he stole another kiss before he answered. "Yes. All that…shit. You're very calm about this." He smiled. "You're neat. Do people still say that?"

Paul buried his face against his chest again. "Not for, like, thirty years. You know, I'm so freaked that I can't even. I'm just gonna roll with it like the mugging."

The lack of instinct for self-preservation continued to amaze Taviano. He was confident that his demon posed no risk to Paul, but the man was a menace to himself. "I'm grateful you aren't throwing me out, but I can't help wishing you showed a little more caution. You won't always have a ninja on hand to help out."

Paul snorted. "It's not like I'm a thrill junkie or anything. I just try to keep it one hundred. I don't want to live in fear. TBH, it goes wrong sometimes, but people are mostly all right, if you trust them."

"Tee bee aytch?"

"To be honest."

"Oh." Had he and Gero spoken in such slang that he just didn't recall? A question for another time. He focused instead on Paul. "You're a remarkable young man."

That earned a full scoff. "C'mon, you've got to be right about the same age as me." Eyes widened again. "Oh shit, that's probably not true. How old are you?"

Taviano considered the question. "I was born one hundred and ninety-four years ago. My body died when I was twenty-two."

Paul opened and closed his mouth several times like a fish on a dock. Shook his head. "Nope. Can't make that compute. I'm twenty-four so let's say we're the same age."

"Is there anything else you'd like to ask?" Once the floodgates were open, Taviano found it tantalizing to confess the whole of his existence. Hundreds of things he'd never said to a living person, and he wanted to say them to Paul. Of course he would make it all go away so the risk was minimal. Yet the lure of unguarded conversation was nearly as intoxicating as Paul's scent.

Paul flashed a grin at him. "Dude, so many questions. But I have a big one first. You ready?" Taviano smiled and nodded. "You wanna make out with me some more?"

He laughed and let Paul's innate happiness and determined rejection of reality sweep him up. The respite from decades of shadow and alleys and solitude was a gift that would sustain him for a long time. He would not hurry to end it.

He was talking. Touching. *Kissing.*

Paul's joy was contagious, and Taviano pulled them together again to spring across the small room. Twisting smoothly in mid-air, he landed on his back lengthwise along the futon. Paul ended up cradled on his chest like a kitten.

He choked out, "That was so *fucking* cool," and then kissed Taviano, squirming and tugging on his black hair. Long, pleasurable moments passed.

Finally they relaxed again and Paul rested his head on Taviano's shoulder. Body heat soaked into Taviano. It reminded him of a day he'd lazed on the bank of the Volturno River in the sun with Gero's head across his belly.

"This is the best date of my entire life," Paul murmured.

"Is that what this is? A date?"

He shrugged. "I don't know what else to call it. It doesn't feel like a hookup."

"I don't know that term. Is it like getting picked up?"

"Sorta. It's just two horny guys low-key fooling around or fucking and then going on about their day. No strings, just sex."

"Do you like that? Having sex with, er, no strings?"

Paul tucked his head under Taviano's chin as he muttered,

"It's what I get. It's all good, though. I enjoy sex and besides, it isn't like anyone wants to date a guy who cooks in a diner."

Taviano stroked his hair. He didn't need his sensitive ears to pick out the tinge of sadness in Paul's words. "I can tell you are far more than that." He tugged Paul's chin up until he could see those blue eyes again. Firmly, he announced "I've decided I'd rather be on a date with you than in a hookup. You should know, however, that I've never gone on a date before."

"Never? Man, you're so lucky. I used to be the *goat* at dates," Paul enthused. "Greatest of all time. Goat. Get it?"

"I do, and I admire your modesty." They shared a smirk and Taviano asked, "Do we get to kiss more on this date, oh wisest of goats?" His head resonated with the thought, *Please say yes.*

"Oh, totally. But first we should talk a little so it isn't only about your *smokin'* hot body." Paul frowned. "Smoking *cold* body? No, that sounds like I'm a necrophiliac."

Taviano grinned. "I hate to be the one to tell you, but that's closer to the truth than you might care to examine."

"Nope," Paul said firmly. "When you turn this all into a dream, I'm not gonna care about that. I just want you to be all intense and sexy and unable to keep your hands off of me."

"Your request is duly noted. And at least part of that is true." He flipped their bodies until Paul lay on his back and cradled Taviano between his hips. Tracing a finger along the sunrise tattoo, he admitted, "I can't keep my hands off you."

"Please don't try. But it's a date, man. First we converse like mature adults, not horned-up bros gettin' off together."

"Very well. What shall we talk about?"

"So, tell me about you."

"What do you want to know?"

"I'll take 'I'm a freaking vampire' for a thousand, Alex. Go!"

"Who is Alex?" When Paul rolled his eyes again, Taviano

murmured, "Never mind." Instead he talked for a little while, about how it felt to host a demon, what it was like to drink blood ("Horrifying. Delicious."), which myths were correct ("Sunlight.") and which were silly ("Of course I can see myself in a mirror.").

Paul was quiet at first, taking in Taviano's words. He grew restless though, and eventually interrupted. "That's all really wild, but you're talking about this demon like it's something different than you."

"Because it is. It has its own awareness. All the magic comes from it and the older it gets, the more power it has. When I was first turned, it felt like this small, hungry thing. Now it's big, but…I don't know how to explain it. It feels *larger* than my body sometimes, but there's always a core of it I can sense deep inside my gut." He shook his head at the failure of his explanation. "I have my own memories, my own mind. We fight sometimes for control of the body."

Paul pondered for a few moments. "If the vampire-thingy is different than you, I'd rather hear about, well, *you*."

"What do you want to know?"

"You must have a gazillion stories. Wait, I know. Tell me what it was like in Naples back when you were actually my age. Did you have a big family?"

"I had a typical family, I suppose. Three sisters and two younger brothers. My grandfather lived with us too. We had to crowd in to a small house but so did everyone I knew."

"Did you ever have, you know, a guy? Did people do that?"

"I suppose there have always been homosexuals. Otherwise there wouldn't be ancient prohibitions against it."

"Yeah, but I mean, what about you?"

Taviano hesitated for a long moment. He'd never spoken to anyone of what Calogero had meant to him, what it had cost him and what he'd lost. Part of him worried that baring his desires would end as badly as when his father discovered him with Gero. Paul's words about not living in fear played in his head. He drew strength from that credo but asked, "Are you sure you want to hear the story? It's a bit depressing."

Paul said, "You are the sexiest motherfucker I've ever made out with, and you seem like a great guy. Or whatever." He blushed. "I just...I'm interested in *you* more than in your, uh, demon."

"Very well." Taviano rested his elbow to the side of Paul's head and propped his chin on his fist. "I had a friend in Naples, yes. We didn't talk about it in those days, but I was in love with him. We experimented, as I guess people say now. We experimented a *lot*, but we got careless. My father caught us and beat me. He told the boy's family. My friend denied everything, said it was one time, that I led him into it..."

He sighed at the memory and the pain of Gero denying what they meant to each other. Paul murmured supportively. Taviano added, "Anyway, my family said I had to go into seminary and become a priest."

Paul raised his head again. "You weren't kidding about the monastic cell."

"Well, not entirely. No ninja training though." He covered his anguish with the tease, but leaned down to steal a kiss, claiming with it more of Paul's strength. "It broke my heart of course, but being a priest wasn't a terrible choice for me. I always loved going to church and I started helping the parish priest serve Mass as soon as I could. I made my peace with it and studied and prayed. I was a few months away from taking holy orders when I received word that my friend was going to marry."

"That bastard," Paul muttered.

"No, there wasn't any other real choice." Bemused, Taviano

realized he still leapt to Gero's defense. "*Everyone* married, so the news shouldn't have surprised me."

He broke off his story and remembered days of torment. He'd refused to leave his cell or speak to the other seminarians. And then Calogero's face, that last night when he'd slipped out of the seminary. Desperate, burning, he'd gone to Gero's window and begged him to run away. He saw again tear-stained cheeks, and heard excuses. *I can't. This is my family. You knew we'd have to do this one day.*

The refusal still made him ache, more than one hundred seventy-two years later. His wild fantasies of traveling until they found *somewhere* they could live united seemed childish in hindsight. Would things have turned out differently for him if they had left together, that night? Calogero hadn't even been willing to try.

"You didn't, like, have to perform the wedding, did you?" Paul's question startled Taviano.

"What? Oh. No." He stroked Paul's hair. "No, I got drunk instead. I bought a bottle of wine and wandered around the streets of Naples like every lovesick boy does. That was when the vampire found me."

Paul gasped. "No shit?"

"No shit. One minute I looked into the harbor and choked on my misery. The next it grabbed my coat and dragged me to a rooftop." He closed his eyes; he could still recall the terror as the creature threw him to his back and loomed over him.

Through matted hair, a hideously white face with burning eyes and sharp, sharp teeth glared down at him. The beast crouched low and plunged his fangs into Taviano's neck. He held Taviano effortlessly with just one of his arms as he lapped up blood with a rough tongue.

His mind rebelled against the impossibility. He couldn't move or cry out. His guts, twisted in fear, already understood what sort of predator had him. The pain was terrible, as was the knowledge that he would die and never see Calogero again. The moon over the vampire's head dimmed and he felt his heart stutter and fail. He was so weak that he couldn't even try to get away.

Suddenly the vampire stopped drinking and pulled back his head. "The demon wants you," he hissed. Curiosity showed in his dark eyes. "Fine. But you will serve me." He slashed fangs across his own wrist and thrust it savagely against Taviano's mouth.

"Let it in," he ordered. "Drink and become one with the night."

The bitter, metallic taste of blood filled his mouth. Taviano thought he would be sick but swallowed it instead. He drew in spurt after spurt of the heated stuff, letting the creature fill him with its darkness and power. By the time the vampire pulled away, Taviano grasped what had happened. Sound beat against his eardrums painfully. The slightest gust of air felt like a razor blade on his skin. The moonlight burned his eyes and he wailed.

"It will pass as you learn," the vampire said coolly, watching his wrist heal. "Embrace what you become, but also understand that I will rend you limb from limb if you disobey me."

Taviano rolled his head side to side, moaning in agony as the blood finished killing him. Another consciousness slithered through his mind, insinuating itself. Something completely separate yet intimate, willful and demanding.

He heard no words but the presence made its drives known. It wanted more blood, more life. It would use Taviano as its instrument and drain the world dry if it could. It hated the other vampire as a threat and a wellspring at the same time. Taviano could feel their relative strength like a throbbing in his gut. He was the weaker one, but his demon let him know that would change over time. It thrummed at him to obey and abide, no matter how much it wanted to rip and rend the creature from which it had come.

And then Taviano died.

His pulse stopped, his legs stilled and he couldn't move his body. But his mind remained aware in his corpse. After a time that might have been eons or minutes, the sound of a huge drum began inside his chest as his heart beat again. It forced the substance that was no longer blood through his arteries, bringing strength and movement back to his limbs. Strength, yes, but no warmth.

"Did you see your boyfriend again?" Paul asked, and Taviano realized he'd told the story aloud. He hadn't meant to do that.

He shook his head. "No. The vampire—his name was Bronislav—forced me onto a ship departing Naples that very night. It was many, many years until I was strong enough to break free of him. I made my way back to Naples at last, to find that my family had all died or emigrated. There was no trace of my friend at all. This was at the start of the great migration of Italians to the United States. By that time many had already begun to leave." Taviano was quiet for a time. He added softly, "I often prayed that he was able to find a new life somewhere."

"I hope he was sorry," Paul whispered as he wrapped his arms tightly around Taviano's waist. "I hope he thought about you every day and felt bad about the choice he made." There was sadness and resignation to Paul's tone.

Taviano lifted his head from the fist on which it rested. "Is there a story you'd like to tell me?"

Paul shook his head. "No. Thank you but I don't want to talk about that now." He shifted their bodies so that he splayed along the length of Taviano and claimed his mouth again. The kiss felt like sympathy at first, but became more. Paul's velvety tongue explored his mouth and the heat of his erection burned like a firebrand. His exploration was intense. The way Paul rutted against Taviano's leg, the heady smell of his arousal and phero- mones, told him Paul would do far more than kiss.

As they shared their lips, Taviano ached to surrender to Paul's desire and return it. He could use his fingers and tongue to show Paul how special he was, how valued. Maybe Paul would want to feel him press inside? It had been a literal age since he considered that part of his anatomy. Everything *could* work as it had when he was alive, with a little focus. If Paul asked for it, Taviano would let himself grow erect.

And then what? The shame instilled almost two hundred years earlier bit at him. *Could I make love to a man before I force him to forget everything we did? How would that be right?* Aghast at the venal impulse, he pulled back.

As if he'd heard Taviano's thoughts, Paul begged, "Please don't make me forget how wonderful this is."

Covering his turmoil, Taviano vowed, "I'll leave you with a good story." He had to be satisfied and not reach for more. Light, friendship, even passion—Paul had already given those unstint- ingly. Grateful and moved, he murmured, "Merry Christmas."

"Christmas." Paul stiffened abruptly. He twisted his body under Taviano's as he craned his neck to find a clock. "Oh fuck, it's so late." He squirmed free and jumped off the futon. "The shelter will close down."

Taviano ached instantly for the loss of his warmth. Its absence made him aware that the ice in his vein had melted a bit while he'd held Paul to him. He shook his head. *I'm ridiculous. I feel body heat from every victim.*

But his victims never simply gave their warmth, the way Paul did.

Paul bustled around the small room, dragging open drawers to pull out a red sweatshirt, clean pants and boxer shorts. He tore off his corduroys and tossed them in a corner before stripping his mistletoe underwear. Taviano glimpsed more of Paul's creamy skin, the pale moon of his buttocks, and tantalizing flashes of more ink. He ached to stroke those tattoos and feel Paul react as he worshipped each mark.

Temptation flared. He could compel Paul to stay with him, to put off delivering the presents. It would be so easy. Just a little nudge of magic and Paul would forget about the shelter until morning...

Chagrin burned Taviano's gut. How could he consider anything so selfish, when Paul had been nothing but open and generous? It was grim enough that he would have to take away Paul's memories at the end of their time together. He could persuade himself that act was ultimately for Paul's own peace of mind. To abuse Paul's trust, just so that Taviano could prolong their intimacy? The thought was abhorrent.

Dressed again, Paul hopped around to get into his boots. "Shit, dude! We gotta go. Maybe it's not too late."

Taviano stamped firmly on his regret and rose from the futon. He scooped up all four bags to follow Paul out of his studio and back into the cold Boston night.

FIVE

AS THEY STARTED up the dark street, Taviano frowned. "You weren't wearing a coat before, and you don't have one now. Aren't you freezing?"

"No, Mom," Paul said with a sardonic glance. "I got rolled for my ski jacket a few weeks ago and I haven't had the cash flow to replace it." He shrugged. "I force how cold I am out of my head."

Not entirely, though; Taviano could sense his shivers. Well, that was something he'd take care of, once he put Paul under and rewrote his memories of the night. Helping himself to cash from one of the drunken men who poured out of expensive bars would be child's play. He'd leave the money for Paul, along with a recollection that he'd won it in a poker game.

There was no rush, though. The night was far too special to end things, at least until the gift escapade ran its course. He wanted to see Paul's expression as he passed presents to the needy children at the shelter. Maybe he could join in the simple pleasure of giving and receiving that he'd lost long ago?

In the meantime, he could help with the cold, for a short time at least. He stopped Paul and, setting down the bags of presents, asked, "Do you trust me?" Paul looked at him and swallowed. Nodded.

"Don't worry, it's nothing bad." Taviano slid a hand up Paul's shoulder until it tangled in blond hair. His demon was remarkably cooperative that evening. When Taviano was sure of its mood, he let a small stream of its magic slip through his fingers. He spoke silently to the icy breeze and bid it wrap around Paul's torso. "Be warm," he whispered and the shivering ceased instantly.

Paul's jaw dropped open and his eyes again resembled saucers. "Man, what did you do? I feel like it's eighty degrees out and I should be in shorts."

"It won't hurt you. I made the air responsive to that strong will of yours. Since you're working so hard to convince yourself that you're warm, you made the air cooperate."

"So it's, like, willpower? I'm like Green Lantern?"

"I don't know what that means."

"You know, the superhero? He has a space ring and whatever he dreams up, his ring forms out of green energy. Didn't you see that shitty movie a few years ago?"

"I rarely go to movies. Too much close contact is risky if I haven't fed."

Paul looked at him blankly. "Oh. Right. Vampire. I kind of forgot already." He frowned. "Did you start making me forget?"

Taviano shook his head. "No. I'm enjoying myself too much. We'll do that after you accomplish this project of yours."

"But..." Paul looked down at the ground.

"Yes?"

"Can we have a real goodbye first? I mean, I don't want you to just whammy me and go away." Taviano could sense extra warmth rise to Paul's cheeks as he flushed. "I don't want to forget at all."

"It's for the best. I promise, though. I won't 'whammy' you until we get a proper goodbye."

Paul seemed to accept that, but didn't talk as he resumed hurrying down the street. He moved too fast and slipped on a patch of ice. Taviano helped steady him and adjusted the bags to one hand so he could give support around the hazards.

The deserted sidewalk stretched ahead for many blocks, he could tell. He had an idea for lightening the mood between them. *Why not?* The strange night brought out mischief in him that felt wrong and right at the same time. He grinned at Paul before gathering him closely and speeding up.

The pavement flew by under their feet as they ran faster and faster. When Paul stumbled slightly, Taviano swept him into his arms and kept running. Paul gave a jubilant cry and wrapped his arms around Taviano's back. "Left!" he called out, and they altered their trajectory.

The chilly, fresh air whipped Paul's hair, but he kept his shining gaze on the road. Still no one was ahead for a good two blocks so Taviano gathered himself and leapt to the top of a brick wall. He ran along it like a cat as far as he could, until the wall ended and he had to jump back down to the pavement.

At the sound of voices in the near distance, he slowed to a human pace and let Paul put his feet to the ground once more. Paul panted next to him and a quick glance showed his eyes shining with excitement. "Dude! That was...so amazeballs. Flying! We flew!" He buried his face in Taviano's neck, seemingly overcome with his emotions.

"Not really, we just ran very fast. I can't actually fly."

"Sucks for you," Paul murmured into his neck. "I want to kiss you again so badly right now."

The desire rising from his skin mixed with the scent of rosemary and lemon to make Taviano's mouth water. His demon stirred and took notice but seemed content to let the moment pass unchallenged.

Hand in hand, Paul directed them down a street lined with trashcans and battered cars but devoid of people. They stopped before a ramshackle townhouse. Someone had draped strands of multicolored lights irregularly across the front of the building. Here and there, a bulb was missing or burnt out. Through a first-story window Taviano could see a Christmas tree encircled with white fairy lights.

All of the windows were otherwise dark, however, and when Paul tried the door, it was locked. His happiness from the journey faded rapidly.

"Shit, shit, shit," Paul berated himself. "I got carried away and now it's all ruined." He kicked at the concrete stair and stuffed his hands in his pockets.

Taviano heard the edge of tears in his voice, and sensed shivers again. Frustration eroded Paul's ability to ignore the icy air, even with Taviano's little trick. The loss of his innate joy alarmed Taviano in a way he'd never experienced. They'd known each other for mere hours. For no reason he could identify, Paul's happiness had become important to him.

More than anything, he wanted to restore the light to Paul's eyes.

He looked over the dark façade with its glowing streaks of color as Paul leaned against him. The surrounding cocoon enveloped Taviano as well. He hadn't felt so warm since he was in New Orleans three, no, four years earlier. It wasn't entirely about the stimulated air molecules, though.

He longed to wrap his arm around Paul's shoulder. Instead, to re-establish some distance, Taviano took a few steps toward the closed shelter. "This mission seems to be very important to you."

Paul scanned the building as he looked for a way in. Eventually, he said quietly, "I know what it's like to get kicked out for being gay. To wake up alone on Christmas with nothing to eat or look forward to." He turned his gaze to Taviano briefly. "Sometimes people surprise you in a bad way."

"Do you mean your family?"

"Partly. I had a boyfriend too. Tim. We went to Boston College together and started hooking up in freshman year. He was all activist on campus and he kept pushing me to come out to my folks. I knew it was a bad idea. They're old-school Italians. Hell, Mama still goes to Mass every day. Anyway, I thought Tim and I were *together*-together, you know? Not fuck buddies. I wanted to make him happy so I told my folks at Thanksgiving." Paul shook his head regretfully. "It was a shit show. Epic drama. Crying and begging in Italian, the works. Papa said if I didn't renounce my evil lifestyle they would no longer support me. Mama agreed with him. Said it was for my own good.

"I told Tim what had happened and asked if I could stay with him. Move into his dorm room for a while. He made some lame-ass excuse about studying. That's when I figured out I didn't mean as much to him as he meant to me."

Taviano had to stamp down his growing rage at the injustices done to Paul, before he riled up his demon. He kept quiet, though, to let Paul talk.

"So, no more home, no more college, no more boyfriend. I went to a shelter for a few weeks but I started flipping burgers and making breakfast at a little diner. It let me scrape enough together to rent my apartment. I moved in on Christmas Eve and when I woke Christmas morning, I had, like, one apple in the fridge." He was silent for a long while before saying quietly, "That was a bad day."

Taviano hated anything that made the exuberant and shining young man sad. He reached for Paul and drew him close. "It sounds very lonely. You strike me as a man who thrives in a crowd."

Paul nodded, and his voice was thick with emotion when he spoke again. "I guess that's true, but I didn't know it until I was on my own. Family was super important growing up. Every Sunday there was a big dinner at my nonna's. Every birthday or little milestone was an excuse for tons of cousins to get together and hang out. Sometimes I just wanted to be by myself, but as soon as a party started up, I'd be right there in the middle. Then my parents tried to cut me off from all that because I was different and it embarrassed the fuckers." A glint appeared in his eye. "Funny thing, though. The cousins still invite me to shit, and my nonna sends me a little money when she can."

"Does this have anything to do with the tattoo on your back? The tree with the missing branch?"

"Yeah, I was salty at them kicking me out, so the tat was a big ol' fuck-you. See, I realized I'm still part of the bigger fam, no matter what the 'rents want. They cut themselves out of my life, but I'm in the story with all these other great people anyway."

After a pause, Taviano asked, "What happened to Tim?"

"He stayed in college after he canceled me. Went on to law school. I never unfriended him on Facebook. If I want to make myself miserable I look at pictures of his life and his perfect new boyfriend."

"Would you like me to eat him?"

Paul shot him an astonished look and Taviano returned a grin. After making sure it was a joke, Paul finally laughed too. Some of the tension that had crept into his bones seemed to ease. "Could you maybe give him some bad dreams?"

"Of course. We'll have him chased by a vampire while he's completely naked."

Satisfied that he'd restored a little of Paul's smile, Taviano extended his senses. He listened for movement inside the shelter, evidence that someone was awake who they could draw to the door. No good, though. Everyone seemed to be asleep. The street also remained unoccupied by people or passing cars.

Paul sighed. "I guess I can come back in the morning and bring the gifts then. No, shit, I have to work the breakfast rush so it'll be afternoon before I can swing by."

Taviano resolved to take away the rest of Paul's unhappiness if he could. "Give me your sweatshirt," he said as he began to undo the buttons down the front of his own black shirt.

"What? Whoa. Are you, like, stripping for me?"

"Not exactly. You'll be warm enough in this and I should wear red. It's the way of the Christmas ninja," Taviano said with a grin. As Paul pulled the sweatshirt over his head, Taviano unbuttoned his cuffs, slipped the shirt off his shoulders, and offered it.

When he stood bare-chested, Paul looked at him with mouth hanging open as his desire perfumed the bubble of warm air. "Oh my *god*," he sighed as his eyes moved over Taviano's body like a caress. "You are just...I mean, I know how you felt through your clothes, but I've never seen someone this cut and defined and fucking perfect."

Taviano looked down at his own chest. Whorls of dark hair covered the slabs of his pectorals, lead to his navel and disappeared into his pants. He rarely thought about his own body as anything more than a vessel for the bloodbeast. He couldn't deny a thrill of pleasure that Paul liked it, though he just shrugged, embarrassed. "Like I said, one of the perquisites."

"That's a major-ass perk." Paul shook his head. "I could kill myself at the gym every day for ten years and never get abs like these." He reached out boldly to run his hand over Taviano's tautly rippled belly and to splay over his chest. He rested his palm right in the sharp cleft in the middle and murmured, "Oh shit. I feel it, like you said." He paused and squinted. "It's different than a heartbeat. More…forceful?"

The warm hand on Taviano's chest stirred something in his carefully regulated core. Softly, he said, "It has to be strong to move the ichor through my body and keep it functioning. Ichor is thicker than human blood." He waited for Paul to show fear or draw away at the reminder of what he touched. The fog of pheromones tinged with rosemary just grew stronger.

Taviano donned Paul's sweatshirt, which was tight on his bigger frame and strained at the shoulders and across his chest. Paul shook his head slowly. "So unfair, but you should always go tight shirt for the dub."

"I won't even ask."

"Dub is a win. You rock my clothes, bruh. That's my new aesthetic." Paul ran his palm to Taviano's shoulder, curled it around his neck and pulled him into another kiss.

Maybe it was the ensorcelled bubble of air around them, but his lips tingled as shivers raced down his spine. The kiss left him full of wonder. "Hold that thought," Taviano said as he reluctantly broke away.

While Paul put on his black shirt, he hoisted the bags of gifts and measured the three-story façade with his eyes. "Step back," he cautioned, aware that he was showing off but telling himself it was just to make Paul happy.

Coiling his legs like a cat, he released a daring burst of his demon's magic and exploded upward. As he hurtled at the roof, he worried briefly that it was too high, that he would fall back to Earth and shame himself. But then a tremendous updraft roared from below. It pushed him the last few feet, wind whistling past his ears, until his toes cleared the edge. He landed neatly on the roof.

Glancing down, he found Paul's face shining at him from the dark street, his arms spread wide for joy. Taviano crouched low and ran lightly over the shingles as he searched for a way in. Soon enough, he found a locked doorway that let out onto the roof, and snapped the handle off easily and quietly. He was able to enter unimpeded by the barrier magic. As with Paul's building, the shelter evidently admitted too many people for it to be a sanctuary.

The steady breathing and occasional snoring of eighteen scattered humans came to him from throughout the shelter. He listened intently and realized at least one—no, three—had awoken in their beds, possibly at his entrance. After the amount of power Taviano had drawn, his demon stirred hungrily. He wasn't confident about releasing more magic to influence anyone who might see him. Its tolerance of Paul might not extend to the residents.

He eased down the stairs as quietly as he could. Probing ahead, he identified and avoided a few treads with weaknesses that might squeak if he stepped on them. The doors on the second floor were ajar and led into what looked like dormitories. Bunk beds lined the walls, and bodies lay in various outlines under thin blankets.

On the first floor he found the common areas—dining room, kitchen, and living room. A large, artificial Christmas tree dominated the front of the house. A few packages lay scattered underneath, but his senses told him they contained little more than candy and nuts.

He began to unload the gifts Paul had purchased, hurrying around to arrange the colorfully wrapped gifts beneath the tree. The candy canes he draped over its boughs. When the bags were empty, he wadded them to tuck under the tree skirt for convenience.

Hands on his hips, Taviano surveyed the results and wished he could show it to Paul. The transformation was spectacular.

Instead of the small assortment of presents, a glorious pile of happiness waited for the residents to unwrap.

The last thing he did was locate a piece of paper and a pen to scribble a note.

> *The chimney was too small for my belly. I'm sorry about the door to the roof but this should cover the repairs.*
>
> *—Love, Santa Claus*

He left the note with some folded money he had in his pocket before slipping up the stairs again.

On the second floor where the residents slumbered or tossed in their beds, Taviano paused. He grinned as he imagined what Paul would do, were he there. *Should I?* He tested the demon's attitude, and found it hungry but not starving. It seemed amenable.

Carefully, he summoned a morsel of its magic. With it he wove a little glamour until the dust motes whipped and swirled around. Red lint from Paul's sweatshirt joined the small tornado he shaped with his mind until it was wider around the middle. If residents came out of their rooms right then, they would see a blurred, red, man-shaped figure with a big belly.

The creature rolled over but seemed…amused? Was that right? Encouraged, he drew a little more power to call clean, cold air over the roof and down the staircase. It brought the scent of snow to his playful illusion. He could tell when a few of the residents woke at the unusual sound and freshening smell. Then one or two more stirred sleepily.

He let out a hearty "Ho, ho, ho" and waited in the middle of his swirling mass, poised to run. Some of the braver souls tumbled out of their rooms to check on the commotion. He waited a split second for them to notice his glinting red shape. At the first sharp gasp, he rushed away at vampire speed. Down the hall and up the stairs to the roof, he pulled the mass of twinkling air with him. Finally, he ran back and forth in a line over the shingles, striking his feet heavily several times.

One of the inhabitants started to follow him to the roof. Taviano could scent the wood of a baseball bat. *Fair enough—time to go.* He ran at the edge of the roof and leapt off. An instant later the door banged open and a trembling but determined male voice yelled, "Get outta here, asshole."

Taviano landed before an astonished Paul, swept him in his arms, and sped away. Floodlights hit the area where Paul had waited. Every window in the townhouse came on. He took them far enough to stay in the shadows and set Paul on his feet. With a finger to Paul's lips, he listened to the ruckus from inside.

Don't see anyone... Nothing missing... Anyone hurt, or see who it was... Charlie, look! Presents... Where did all this shit come from... This has my name on it ...

He smiled and pulled Paul to him for a passionate kiss before explaining what he'd done. "They're finding your gifts now."

Paul hugged him back blissfully. "Oh man, I'm gonna kiss you so hard. You actually gave them Santa Claus!"

Taviano flushed slightly at the reaction, yet he was grateful to have restored Paul's happiness. Something unexpected occurred to him. He'd never before used his abilities to help someone. To bring a little joy, as he had with his Santa tricks.

The warmth that idea produced in some ways rivaled what he'd felt when Paul was in his arms, back in the apartment. Every use of power that he recalled had been for the demon's own hungers. He'd tracked prey or fed or concealed its monstrosity. Claiming a little of that magic for himself, directing it to help instead of harm, made him straighten his spine.

Of course he'd done everything to please Paul, but the fact that the bloodbeast permitted it… That was something to contemplate on lonely nights after he'd left Boston and Paul behind.

Pride gave way to chagrin as he admitted, "I probably scared a lot of them too. I hope they'll understand I did no real harm."

"Fuck 'em if they can't take a joke." Paul waved away the concern. "What was that noise at the end, before you jumped back down?"

Taviano looked at the ground and scuffed it with his toe. "Well, I wanted to make a sound that might, to a city child, resemble reindeer."

At that, Paul doubled over with his laughter. "I'm weak! What a trip. 'The prancing and pawing of each little hoof.' And the red swirly stuff." He could hardly breathe. "When you jumped you should have yelled, 'Merry Christmas to all and to all a good night'!"

"I would have but a man with a baseball bat was on his way. I didn't think he'd see the humor." Paul's laughter was infectious, and Taviano found himself grinning from ear to ear. "I'm glad that you do." He cocked his head at the townhouse. "Everyone's awake now. Do you want to knock on the door so they can thank you?" When Paul shook his head, he asked again, "Are you certain?"

"Hundo-p," Paul exclaimed as he straightened and tried to get himself under control. "That means I'm one hundred percent sure. I don't need them to know where the presents came from. Besides, I didn't really even buy 'em. It was donations." His eyes shone adoringly at Taviano. "I'm not going to take a moment of Santa away from the kids. Best. Christmas. Ever."

As if to underline the point, it began to snow.

SIX

TAVIANO SENSED THE first flakes drifting down toward them, descending on their adventure like a benediction. Paul followed Taviano's gaze skyward and snow brushed his face. He spread his hands wide, sticking out his tongue to catch it.

Sharing laughter on a snowy night after decades alone felt like a reward and a punishment all in one. Taviano was happier in that moment than he could ever recall, basking in Paul's light. Yet some part of him warned the years stretching ahead would be that much darker by comparison. He wanted to extend the evening forever, but he could sense the cocoon around Paul starting to dissipate.

"We should get you home," he said regretfully. "You're losing the warm air."

Paul sobered as he brushed snow from his eyebrows. "Boo. I don't want to go home yet. Can't you just juice me again?"

Taviano considered his demon's unusual reaction to Paul but still shook his head. "It isn't worth the risk to you. My demon is hungry and a little restless. When I draw on its power like I did for you and to create my illusion in the shelter, I give it an opening. It's a constant effort to keep it locked down. The hungrier it is, the harder time I have. If it escaped… Well."

That sucked the mood out of the dark alley where they stood.

Paul's brow furrowed and in a hushed voice, he asked, "Would you kill me? I mean, would *it* kill me?"

"So far it's shown no interest in feeding on you," Taviano admitted, "but it might try. In any case the amount of blood needed to satiate a bloodbeast isn't enough to kill a healthy adult. If I let it feed, it usually calms enough for me to force it back. Afterward I make the victim forget, do my trick with the wounds, and move on. But I don't always succeed in controlling it."

"From Santa Claus to *The Nightmare Before Christmas*," Paul murmured. Taviano looked away. In a stricken voice, Paul exclaimed, "Oh god, I'm sorry. That was super mean. I don't really think that."

Taviano sounded hoarse to himself as he said, "You did. And I understand. I'm a monster after all." He squinted at the sky. "It's past midnight. Let's get you home and I can make you forget all of this." He pulled off the red sweatshirt and offered it to Paul, who returned his thin black shirt.

Dressed in their own clothes again, Paul tugged down his hem and looked ashamed of his outburst. "Taviano, I'm sorry. I don't want it to end this way. With you mad at me." More quietly, he said, "I don't want it to end at all." He took Taviano's hand and they began to walk back in the direction of Paul's apartment.

Taviano could have whisked them there in moments, but he found he didn't want the night to end either.

A few blocks into their stroll, Paul asked, "Are you…? Wow, this is a weird question." He stopped himself, but then spit it out anyway. "Do you live here in Boston? I mean, do you have, like, a den or something here?"

"No." Taviano could feel Paul waiting for more, and a block later he gave it to him. "I never stay in one place more than a single night, and rarely in an area more than a few days. I always move on."

"For almost two hundred years? That's like…" Paul squinted as he seemed to work out the math.

Taviano sighed. "It's been sixty-two thousand, eight hundred fifty-three nights since Bronislav turned me."

Paul clutched his hand harder. "Sixty-two *thousand* nights of traveling? Of never knowing where you're going to be next? Isn't that exhausting?"

"If I let myself dwell on it, yes. I've been all over Europe and Asia. Africa. South America. I've walked the length and breadth of North America alone four times over. When I get tired of America, I might go to Australia next." Paul apparently processed that as Taviano continued. "I'd like to go to Antarctica though I doubt I could keep my demon fed. Not enough people there, and I hate the idea of drinking from a penguin or other fauna I might find. Animal blood doesn't work very well anyway."

"Why do you never stay in one place?"

"That was how Bronislav trained me, to move constantly. I was practically his slave for years after he turned me. When I was finally free of him, I had no better plan so I kept going. Vampires are extremely solitary, you see.

"I'm not sure whether this will make any sense to you. When two of us meet, the bloodbeasts become practically unhinged with the need to destroy and consume each other. With a newly turned vampire, it's manageable. It has to do what its sire tells it, no matter how much they hate each other. When both vampires are mature, though, a battle can erupt, and if it does, it's violent and destructive and reckless. The solution—I guess you'd call it a custom—has developed among our kind. Once a vampire claims a territory, others mostly respect it and stay out to avoid a fight. Rarely, a vampire decides to take a territory. Then there *is* a battle that doesn't end until one kills the other."

"Wait, a vampire can die?" Paul interrupted.

"We call it the second or final death. Sunlight, fire, the loss of all ichor—these and a few other things can kill a bloodbeast. When it dies, so does the vampire host. But those battles are rare."

"Have you ever tried to take a, what did you call it? A territory?"

Taviano shook his head. "I've never found any place I wanted to claim for myself. I just move constantly, slipping across the edges, avoiding encounters." He shrugged. "It doesn't always work but for the most part I've been able to stay out of fights or get away when they erupt."

"Are there other vampires here? Is this someone else's place?"

"Oh yes. Big cities like Boston and New York and Chicago are divided among a few vampires. The population is dense enough to support more than one bloodbeast, as long as they keep some distance from each other. Out in the western parts of America—in Montana for example—one or two vampires may claim the entire state."

"Do you have to, uh, feed every night?"

"No. Unless I've expended a lot of energy I can go three or four days, which gives me time to be selective." Taviano dipped his head sheepishly. "This sounds pretentious, but I look for the worst. I wait in the roughest part of a town or a city and watch. When I'm sure a person is bad enough, I stalk him. Then I get him alone..."

"And you drink blood from him," Paul finished quietly. "Whoa. That's some heavy shit."

Their walk had brought them back to St. Stephen's. The sounds of another service taking place, surely midnight Mass given the late hour, made Taviano pause. He looked at the belfry high above. "I was on the roof there when I spotted the muggers coming after you earlier."

"Lucky for me. Talk about the worst dudes. That could have been bad." Paul stopped next to him, also craning his neck. The muffled sound of a choir carried through the closed doors of the church. Paul must have caught the wistful look on Taviano's face. "Did you, like, go into the church earlier?"

Taviano shook his head. "No. It's forbidden."

Paul wore a puzzled frown. "What does that mean?"

"It means a bloodbeast can't enter a holy sanctuary."

"Holy to whom? And you were on the roof earlier. Why is it different?"

Taviano thought about that. "I don't know. Bronislav never explained, beyond telling me that we couldn't enter a holy place."

"So, like, you never tested it?"

"Of course not," Taviano exclaimed, scandalized. "A church is sacrosanct. I'm hosting a demon that doesn't belong in there."

Paul's eyes scanned the front of the church and moved to the belfry. "There's a big-ass crucifix on top. Does it drive you away? Or make you hurt?"

"Well, no," Taviano admitted cautiously, and Paul snorted.

"You know what? I'm calling bullshit on Bratislava."

"Bronislav."

"Whatevs. Here's what I think." An edge of excitement had crept into Paul's tone, and he bobbed his head briskly. "This demon thing and not entering a holy place and all that is just crap." He twined his arms around Taviano's waist. "You can touch a church. You choose to feed only from bad guys. You gave a bunch of homeless kids Christmas, for fuck's sake." Eyes glinting fiercely, he declared, "You aren't a demon, Taviano. You're an angel."

The words moved Taviano. He didn't believe them for a moment but it was a sweet thing to hear. Still, he shook his head in denial. "I'm a killer."

"Not really. You try not to kill when you eat, even if it's some evil dude. That doesn't sound like a monster to me, any more than a meat eater who survives on cows and pigs is a monster."

Taviano brushed Paul's hair out of his eyes. "I appreciate the way you see me. But you can't feel the thing inside me and what it wants to do. It's completely amoral. Everyone is food."

"Even me?"

That made Taviano pause. "Well, no. For some reason, that isn't how it thinks of you."

"Exactly!' Paul cried, as if he'd proved a point. When Taviano continued to show doubt, he expelled a loud sigh and said in a frustrated tone, "You don't believe me." After a moment's thought, he took Taviano's hand. "Try. For me. As a Christmas present."

"Try what?"

"Let's see how close you can get to the church before you actually feel something, like, pushing back. Or just weird even."

"I don't know…" But he allowed Paul to coax him closer to the building.

"Step by step. Look. The doors are closed." Paul waited for Taviano to join him at the top of the stairs leading to the church. He looked at the sky. "No lightning bolts. No smoke or brimstone." Eyes again on Taviano, he tilted his head. "Do you feel anything different?"

Taviano shook his head slowly. The bloodbeast didn't recoil from proximity to the church. Come to think of it, neither had it recoiled earlier, when he crouched on the belfry. He hadn't noticed then, and still he sensed nothing unusual in the air.

Tentatively he stretched to brush fingers over the wooden doors, ready to pull back at the first burn or pain. Nothing happened. The door was merely wood.

Paul grinned and pulled open the side closest to him. He stepped inside and turned around to face Taviano. "One finger maybe?"

If Taviano's heart could change rhythm, it would pound. The combined scents of the Mass, wafting through the opened door, pulled at his memories. He extended his hand slowly until he broke the plane of the threshold. Nothing like the eldritch, otherworldly force that protected a home interfered at the church door. Clearly too many people went in for the barrier magic to shield the public spaces. Still, Taviano expected the sanctified ground to repel him. At any moment he anticipated searing pain or, well, *something*.

Seconds passed with only his hand in the narthex of the church.

Could it be true?

Paul clasped his wrist and tugged gently, drawing them both inside. Every fiber of Taviano's body was ready to bolt but he remained fine. More confident as the same *nothing* continued to happen, he stepped fully into the church.

The Mass had reached the portion in which the congregation recited the Apostle's Creed. The murmur of a hundred voices echoed around the walls and statues and stained glass windows. "I believe in the Holy Spirit. With the Father and the Son he is worshipped and glorified…," they intoned.

A blinding smile lit Paul's face as he watched Taviano begin to accept. He led them to an empty pew at the rear of the nave and Taviano sank onto it, stunned. A Christmas tree stood at the left of the altar. *Father Francesco would never have permitted such a secular display.* The crèche to the right, however, reminded Taviano of the one in his mother's house.

They remained seated, leg pressed to leg, arm to arm, through the presentation of the offerings. He silently mouthed the prayers in Latin. A profound sense of homecoming tightened in his chest and made his vision blur at the edges.

Rising at a signal from the priest, they stood through the Lord's Prayer, and then seated themselves again. Most of those present filed down to take the wafer and sip the wine as the choir sang jubilantly in the loft.

When the priest instructed the people to exchange a sign of peace, men and women throughout the church shook hands. Taviano turned to Paul, his eyes burning with unshed tears, and kissed him.

"*La pace sia con te*," he whispered, trying to convey everything he felt, with gratitude above all.

Paul answered proudly, "And also with you." He entwined his fingers with Taviano's and held his hand tightly through the final glorious anthems that soared from the choir. When the Mass ended, the priest instructed the congregants to go and celebrate the birth.

They left St. Stephen's ahead of the crowd, and Taviano felt as light as he had when he rushed through the night with Paul in his arms. The snow had ended by the time they emerged and the clouds had begun to part again. Paul dragged Taviano around the building and down Clark Street. The fresh powder coated walls and trashcans and doorsteps, softening the shapes around them and muffling the city noises. They found a dark corner and Paul pulled him into it. Wrapping Taviano in a mighty hug, he whispered excitedly, "I knew it. I knew you aren't a monster."

Taviano hugged him back, but he was still in a sort of shock. "All those long years." Many, many times he'd needed the comfort of the Church and had kept away only on Bronislav's word. What else might his maker have lied about, or not understood himself? He knew some of the things Bronislav had taught him proved wrong or incomplete. So why had he never tested the stricture on holy places?

The answer to that question was obvious: from the start, from his first victim, he'd known he was damned. Like a self-hating fool, he had *accepted* that he was a murderer. A church was *of course* forbidden to him.

Until Paul refused to believe that Taviano was a fiend.

Something rolled down his cheek, tickling his skin. When he wiped at it, his finger came away glistening with a clear substance tinged with blood. "I think I'm crying."

Paul took Taviano's finger and drew it into his own mouth, sucking it clean before Taviano could stop him. "You probably shouldn't have done that," he said with a frown.

Paul grinned cheekily and said, "*Lacrimae mundi.* The tears of the world." He shrugged. "Hey. I went through Confirmation. I remember a few things." Suddenly his grin faltered. "Whoa." His pupils dilated and his heartbeat throbbed. Sweat broke out on his forehead as Taviano drew him closer.

He tried to recall what had happened on the few instances he'd witnessed a human taste ichor. Once, in the sixties, he'd watched from a distance. An unknown vampire stood in the center of a circle of naked men and women. She dripped a single bead of ichor onto each of their tongues. The ensuing orgy had shocked and intrigued Taviano in equal measure.

In his most reassuring tone, he said to Paul, "Don't worry. You're feeling my demon's magic but you had the barest taste. It isn't enough to do any harm, though you're about to feel very odd."

Paul looked at his hands like they were the most fascinating things in the world. "I think...I think I *see* my pulse." He threw back his head suddenly and pivoted left and right. "What am I hearing? Cars. People. A fight." He focused on an apartment across the street and smiled hugely. "Fucking. I hear two people fucking."

Taviano had to laugh. "It takes a lot of focus to sort through the noise and let in what you need. It won't last long."

"My skin tingles. I'm not cold again."

His wonderstruck expression moved Taviano. Paul apparently relished the experience, so he might as well help. Gently, he enfolded Paul in his arms, nudged a finger under his chin, and said, "Take a look at the stars."

Paul tilted back his head and gasped. "All of them," he moaned, sagging against Taviano. "I see all of the stars. The *colors* there. I had no idea." He looked at Taviano again and blinked several times before brushing fingers over his cheek and down his neck. There was awe in his eyes.

"You're glorious," Paul murmured randomly, then, "I'm tripping balls."

"I wish I had a lexicon so I understood what you're saying. Tripping balls—is that good or bad?"

"It's very, very good. Can we fuck?"

SEVEN

"**W**HAT?"

As if Taviano hadn't heard the request clearly. As if he couldn't feel the yearning in the fingertips Paul stroked along his face, or tell that Paul's shaft was hard as stone.

Taviano had been human when he last made love, and that had ended disastrously. The lesson of that final time—when his father had caught, beaten and sent him to seminary—still hurt. The few intervals after that he'd touched for pleasure involved nothing more than fingers or a flick of his tongue. No one since Bronislav turned him had sufficiently stirred his human nature to seek connection.

But then, he'd never met anyone like innocent, strong-willed, funny, fierce, delightful Paul.

Wrapping fingers in Taviano's shirt, Paul pulled him close. "Everything is so intense and wonderful. Your skin kind of glows and your lips are all soft and red. And I bet your cock is gorgeous. I want to feel it on me. *In* me." He ran a thumb over Taviano's cheek and mouth, sparkling eyes scanning his face as if memorizing every detail. Then he dragged Taviano into a molten kiss.

Taviano quickly found himself yielding to the passion and need pouring forth. His doubts from earlier began to seem feeble and unworthy of the trust placed in him.

But no. It couldn't be right to give in to his desires when the taste of ichor affected Paul. He broke the kiss with a gasp and focused on Paul's blown pupils and pounding heartbeat. "It's the magic—"

"I don't care if it's magic or Christmas or the fact that you are the sexiest fucking man I've ever seen in my life. Come home with me, Taviano. Make love with me."

He rested their foreheads together. Paul's openness and refusal to live in fear were marvelous. Taviano may have worried for the safety of his new friend but he admired him too. Paul embraced his nature even though it had cost him.

And what exactly was Taviano afraid of? His family had shoved him aside long ago as well, and they were gone in any case. A night like the one Paul gave him was unlikely to come again. Regret would haunt him if he failed to accept what Paul offered.

Still, he might have refused. He *should* have refused, but then his demon stirred. Not in his belly or his head, but in his groin. With Paul kissing his neck, Taviano's member stretched down the leg of his pants. He grew almost painfully hard. The desire he felt was nothing like the blood hunger that his demon normally radiated. Rather, it seemed to want him to do this for himself. Paul licked up behind his ear, and the shiver of pleasure made his prick flex.

"I can't resist you both," Taviano gasped.

Sweeping Paul into his arms, he raced through the shadowed streets. Paul clung to him, kissing his face and hair as they ran. Taviano probed ahead as they neared Paul's alley and kept running. He jumped to the single-story roof of a garage, and reversed course to leap onto a second-floor fire escape. Another shift. They flew to the roof of the building that faced Paul's apartment before crossing the chasm to his window ledge.

Barely pausing, Taviano pushed open the narrow sash and levered them both inside. A moment to close it again, and he gave himself over to passion.

Pausing the frantic kisses, Paul asked, "How did you know that window would open?"

"I spotted the broken lock when we were here earlier. I planned to fix it when I—" He choked off what he started to say.

Paul pulled back. "When you make me forget."

Taviano nodded, half-expecting the admission to end whatever was between them. Instead, Paul ripped open his shirt. Buttons bounced away into the darkness as he growled, "Don't you *dare* make me forget one second. This is the most fantastic night of my life and I don't want it hidden away in a dream."

He gave Taviano no time to answer but tugged and pulled until they fell onto his futon. His fingers at the waist of Taviano's pants were nimble as he unfastened, unzipped and shoved them down in seconds. Taviano helped Paul remove his sweatshirt and jeans, and tugged off his ragged boxers.

Their naked bodies pressed together, Paul on top, chest against chest, bellies tight. Mouths locked into a kiss and their hips shifted enough to fit. Hard, hard cocks rubbed and leaked as they glided against one another. Paul wove one hand into Taviano's thick hair and reached for Taviano's shaft with the other. When he wrapped fingers around it, he broke off the kiss with a gasp to look down.

"Of course you'd have a humongous cock too," he moaned. "Thank god for Italian genes. Your stuff leaking out..." He swiped his thumb over the plump head. "Is it the same as your tears? Is it that ichor stuff?"

When Taviano nodded, Paul raised his thumb to his mouth and licked it clean. Closing his eyes, he said softly, "Ohhhh. It tastes like honey and the sea and my birthday all at once." He shot an alarmed look at Taviano. "Should I not…? I mean, how much before it gets dangerous?"

Taviano licked the faintest trace of himself from Paul's lips. "Before you become like me? Don't worry. I would have to drain nearly all of your blood to the point of death and feed it back to you before you'd change. And even then, I believe it only works if the bloodbeast wants it to happen. I've never actually transformed anyone myself."

Paul blinked several times. "Wow. There's a lot to unpack in that statement so I'm gonna focus on the part I like." He grinned wickedly. "I can swallow as much of your come as I want."

He slid down the futon, gently biting at Taviano's nipples. Again Taviano expected discomfort as Paul's stubble grazed over the muscles of his chest. Yet he no longer felt surprise it didn't come. Perhaps the lust between them turned sensitivity to pleasure, or the passing decades had inured him. Maybe it was simply the wonder of *Paul*; Taviano had no idea.

And he couldn't care less about the reason. He groaned at Paul's teeth dragging over his skin. Paul traced his tongue down to Taviano's navel and raised a hand to cup his balls. Rolling them firmly, he licked the muscle where abdomen met groin. He shifted to make Taviano spread his legs further, and slid his warm tongue along the crease between thigh and sac. It took Taviano moments to realize what he intended.

"Are you going to…? Good lord," he gasped as Paul sucked one testicle into his mouth. Paul used his teeth to press lightly on the orb while caressing it with his tongue. He repeated the exquisite torture on the other ball, as Taviano's prick stretched up. It was long and thick, harder than it had ever been. He ached.

Paul rose to his knees, wrapped fingers tightly around the base of Taviano's erection. When he lapped at the clear juices dripping from its head, Taviano fought to hold himself still. Yet his hand crept to rest on the back of Paul's neck. Their eyes met and Paul's glinted roguishly as he lowered his mouth.

Taviano groaned. The warmth and the wetness surrounding him were like nothing he could recall. Gero had never wanted to try, though he'd liked it when Taviano pleasured him with his lips and mouth. Paul, though… Paul was enthusiastic and, as far as Taviano could tell, quite skilled.

Paul ran his tongue over the head and slid it under the retracted foreskin. He nibbled lightly down Taviano's fat length to the root. He nuzzled his scrotum and sucked on each ball again, one at a time. Then he flattened his tongue to run up the thick ridge beneath his prick. Returning attention to the head, he licked off welling juices. Taviano moaned as Paul slid the helmet-shaped tip back into his mouth. He bobbed his head as he worked eagerly to take Taviano further down.

Maybe the ichor worked its magic to soothe the way. Soon Paul's lips pressed to Taviano's coarse, dark hair and his cock was impossibly deep in Paul's throat. It pulsed and throbbed there, against the delicate tissues.

Paul came off it with a gasp and his eyes blazed at Taviano. His heartbeat sped even more, his pulse ratcheted, and his own shaft flexed between his bent legs. "I just realized," he said breathlessly. "You can fuck me raw."

"You're talking about condoms, yes? I…I don't know about that." Taviano considered as he combed his fingers through Paul's shaggy, soft hair. "I suppose so. I can't get or transmit human diseases. The ichor heals—"

"Do it," Paul said eagerly. Intently. "I want you to fuck me and come inside me." Taviano must have looked doubtful because Paul shook his head. "This isn't the ichor or whatever talking. Yes, I'm fucking high but at the same time I'm not. I've *been* high, dude, where I'm drifting and making bad decisions and nothing seems real."

He lightly twisted the skin of Taviano's rigid prick again until Taviano hissed in pleasure. "This isn't like that at all. It's amazing but I'm still me. And I want to feel you come."

His demon was there too, egging him on. He demurred one more time. "Paul, you have to understand. It isn't semen I produce. It's all ichor and blood."

If anything, Paul's pupils blew wider with lust. "Blood and magic and *you*." He shifted onto his back and tugged until Taviano nestled in the cradle between his legs. "You're my Christmas angel, Taviano. Please give me this."

An angel. His word seemed ridiculous to a vampire. He haunted dark streets and preyed on humanity but, oh, it stirred Taviano to hear. The way Paul saw him, as an uncanny guardian, was as seductive as the lean and beautiful body splayed for him. All the nights he'd taken and drained and even killed, and yet there lay a man *giving* himself to Taviano. No one, not even Calogero, had wanted him so much.

His ability to resist vanished. As Paul pulled his knees back, Taviano fell forward with a groan to press his cockhead against Paul's opening. He hovered there, swiveling his hips so that clear liquid spread all around the tight knot of muscle. His memories of long-ago experiments came to mind and brought concern for Paul's comfort. Before he could say anything, his demon throbbed confidence and assurance at him.

He didn't question his sudden knowledge as he brought his mouth an inch away from Paul's lips. He whispered, "I expect the ichor will help you take me inside. I don't think we need anything more than that and your saliva." Still he hesitated, begging silently for one more sign of resolve.

"Fuck me, Taviano," Paul pleaded with soft eyes and a smile stretching his sweet mouth. "Fill me up. I trust you." He tugged

Taviano's head and rocked his hips eagerly until Taviano pressed forward.

The body beneath him opened to accept his cock as Paul crooned. Heat like the sun Taviano hadn't felt in almost two centuries surrounded his length. It sank through his vampire-sensitive skin to his core. Eyes wet with emotion, he slid steadily, relentlessly into Paul.

"I can't even tell you... Aaaaah," Paul began but broke off with a shiver. He tried again, as he gasped and threw back his head. "There's this incredible stretch and fullness. My brain says I should hurt from how thick you are. Icy." Paul bore down, and Taviano felt his rectum pulse and squeeze around his prick. "Jesus. You're this shaft of, like, cool glass sliding up inside, but right away it goes all smooth and delicious. I love the way it feels in my ass."

He spread his knees wider and put his hands on Taviano's hips to pull him down. "Harder. Please. Give me everything," he pleaded.

And Taviano did. Over one hundred and seventy years had passed since he'd been inside anyone but the movements were primal. His human genes remembered what to do. He bucked and twisted, thrust his hips, stroked the head of his cock along the roof of Paul's passage. He jabbed its fat head against Paul's gland until he gasped. Taviano's senses guided him to every sweet spot on and in Paul's body. He licked behind an ear, trailed fingers along his ribs, loved on a nipple with lips alone. He could tell before Paul did what would make him respond in satisfaction or tighten in potential discomfort. When to thrust faster and what to avoid. He made his lover sob and cry for more.

As his cock tunneled in, Taviano ran his tongue up Paul's chest to his neck. When he lapped along the bottom of his jaw, Paul's hole throbbed again and his breath hitched. He rolled his head to one side, exposing himself. Taviano rested his fangs against the carotid artery, so Paul could feel the pinpricks of his eyeteeth. Gasping with pleasure at the contact, Paul clenched Taviano's hips hard. His fingers would have left bruises on a normal man.

Through his teeth, Taviano could feel the vibration of rushing blood. There was no danger of losing control and piercing the skin. All he wanted was to wring every bit of pleasure for both of them as their passion climbed. Almost in disbelief, he grew harder and more sensitive as he stroked Paul's body from the inside out. Ripples of pleasure began at the head of his cock where it stabbed into Paul. The awe-inspiring sensation spread outward to his muscles and his skin.

"I think I'm going to come," he gasped in amazement as he pressed their foreheads together.

Paul thrust his hips and clenched his hole rhythmically around Taviano's invading shaft. Through gritted teeth, he choked out, "That's the point. Do it inside me. I want everything you'll give me. So deep. Ah god…" He cried out and shuddered as ropes of white shot from his cock and coated his belly and chest.

Taviano lowered his head to lick what he could reach, savoring the taste that wasn't blood but rather the stuff of new life. And then he pounded and exploded, shot and melted inside Paul. He was helpless as spasms shook him to the core.

The pleasure sang through his prick, and even his hair and hands and feet. His whole *body* orgasmed. As one rush subsided, another built and crested, filling his balls again, spurting from his cock and spreading into Paul. Time lost meaning for him. It seemed he held a treasured flower between his hands. He knew he had to protect it even as his pleasure consumed, destroyed, and rebuilt him. Taviano wanted to drown in happiness but instead he rode waves of ecstasy. He was buoyed by the kindness of a mortal man who gave of himself endlessly.

"Paul," he moaned, helpless as yet another bolt of lightning shot through him.

When the pleasure finally ebbed and he returned to himself, Paul gazed at him with shining eyes and a glorious smile. He whispered, "Welcome back," and chuckled at Taviano's face. "Oh man. I think you came over and over for two solid minutes. I've never heard of a man having multiple orgasms. I thought that was, like, for women."

"Another perquisite, I suppose," Taviano said weakly.

"A fucking big one." Paul shivered and squirmed even as he clutched firmly at Taviano to prevent him from pulling out. "I could feel every single spurt in my ass but as much as you shook you were careful." Shyly, he added, "You held me like I was precious through the whole thing."

"You are," Taviano said simply and rested his lips against shaggy blond hair.

Paul closed his eyes and twitched his hips. "I can feel your stuff in me. It's like when you rub IcyHot on your skin or something." He laughed. "Well, you wouldn't know what that is, I guess."

"Like menthol? We used to use that."

"Yeah, exactly! Menthol. It's cool and it's spreading and easing every ache I wasn't even aware of before." Paul quivered, but happily. "Good thing because otherwise I don't think I'd be able to walk straight tomorrow. God, you're fucking big," he groaned, squeezing again around Taviano's member. "This come thing is, like, perfect because it means the sex isn't over. You know? Like, you're still moving in my body and it's calming and soothing."

Taviano's concern for Paul warred with his curiosity. "How is it? Is the additional ichor making you feel strange, or increasing your senses further?"

Paul pondered that, then shook his head. "I don't think so. I still hear things I can tell are far away, and my skin tingles, but I feel sharp and clear." He tugged Taviano down until his weight rested on him. "I feel wonderful," he added with a sigh.

They kissed some more, gently, sweetly. The demon all but purred in Taviano's belly.

EIGHT

THEY LAY ON the futon for a long time with Taviano nestled between Paul's legs, his head on Paul's chest. After a while, he murmured, "You should hear your heart. It's pounding strongly."

"I know, right? It's like, I can feel my pulse and your heartbeat while I'm lying here. The noise doesn't seem overwhelming now but there's a cat two floors down that's hungry."

Taviano was quiet. He didn't want to end the spell that their lovemaking had woven, but he heard a distant clock chime two. He finally said, "I'm going to have to leave soon. Your memories—"

"No, fuck that," Paul interrupted severely. "We already talked about this. I don't want to forget a moment."

"I think it's a bad idea, but I'll respect your decision."

"Thank you." Paul twined his arms more tightly around Taviano. "Do you really have to go?"

Taviano kissed the tip of his nose and nodded. "Sunlight burns. That one I confirmed for myself, when I chose the wrong shelter and a shaft of light hit my skin while I was asleep."

"Huh. It seems weird to think of you doing something as normal as sleeping." He added with a little smile, "Ninjas shouldn't sleep."

Taviano chuckled and carded fingers again through Paul's too-long blond hair. "I seem to have grown addicted to touching you."

Paul arched his head happily against Taviano's fingers and asked, "What happens when you sleep? Do you dream, or know what's going on around you?"

"I do dream, usually about all the places I've traveled. It's been a long time so I may not remember human dreams accurately, but now they're sharp. Vivid. It's more like replaying memories than having fantasies from my subconscious." Taviano brushed his cheek against Paul's. "I suspect I'll dream of you for many years."

"Could you maybe stay here one more day? Like, if I found a room no sun could reach? I'd love to wake up on Christmas morning and know you're near, and I'll see you again come evening."

Taviano sighed. "It's a nice wish, and I thank you for that. But it's too dangerous for everyone. I need to go soon so I can find a place to lair, and I'll move on when I wake." He needed to get Paul some money or a coat as well. Damned if he could figure how to do that without altering Paul's memories. He'd honor his wishes, though. Maybe he should slip back in after Paul slept but before dawn, and leave the items with a note.

Paul raised a finger to Taviano's mouth, nudged up his lip and stroked one of his sharp canines. "Is it about feeding? I'd let you take some of my blood, if it would help."

Oh, you sweet and foolish man. "You don't understand the risk, Paul. When my demon feeds, it's close to the surface. It's very strong. Sometimes I can't force it down in time." He hid his face as he said in a low voice, "People have died."

"Oh. I guess you said that before." Paul tugged on Taviano's chin, and a stubborn gleam showed in his eyes. "I'd take the risk.

I believe you'd never hurt me or let *it* hurt me."

"It's out of the question." Taviano rose from the futon and began to look around for his clothes.

Paul got up as well and brushed a hand over the dried semen matted in his sparse chest hair. "Oof. I should do something about this." He retrieved a towel from the tiny bathroom to wet in the kitchen sink. After scrubbing it across his body, he tossed it aside and yanked on his underwear.

As if Taviano had not already made his intentions clear, Paul murmured, "Y'know, the basement here has storage lockers for each of the apartments. They're big enough to hold a couch, so you could lie down. I was in there one time and it's completely dark. No windows at all. It's not fancy but—"

"Paul, I can't stay," Taviano interrupted gently. He finished dressing as well as he could, with buttons missing from his shirt, then helped Paul settle his sweatshirt. He rested his hands on Paul's shoulders. Quietly, he said, "This has been the best night of the past decades, but it isn't the start of something. It's the end." He cringed at the wounded look Paul gave him before dropping his gaze. "I'm so sorry. I don't want to leave you, but you must understand that this is a fantasy for both of us."

"It's Christmas," Paul said to the floor, his voice thick. "Couldn't we enjoy each other a little longer before we have to face real life?"

The words echoed in Taviano's memory. "You sound like Calogero," he said, and Paul's head shot up.

"Calogero?"

"The friend I told you about, from when I was human."

"You never mentioned his name."

"Didn't I? Anyway, he said something very like that not long before my father caught us and everything changed."

Paul didn't seem to hear him but pulled away to rush over to a battered trunk under one of the windows. "Calogero's a pretty unusual name, isn't it?" he mumbled as he rummaged in the box, shifting things around. "It's here somewhere. I know I packed it."

"I suppose it is. Even in my time, I never heard of another. I believe his parents named him for his grandfather."

"A-ha!" Paul stood with a scrapbook in his hands and began to flip through pages. He stopped at one and turned to meet Taviano's eye. "I was seriously into genealogy and my nonna helped me make this for a Boy Scout project. My great-something on my mother's side immigrated to Boston from Italy. His name was Calogero Alligheri." He offered the scrapbook to Taviano. "I have this one picture of him."

Calogero Alligheri. The name froze Taviano where he stood. It was a ridiculous coincidence. Impossible. Even if he'd never met another man with that name, it couldn't possibly be *his* Gero.

He took the scrapbook with trembling hands and stared at the sepia-toned photograph. In the center, an elderly man in a formal suit stood next to a strong-looking woman with white hair. Surrounding them were other, younger adults, and two babies. All were stiff and posed, dressed finely and unsmiling. The babies wore what appeared to be christening gowns.

"That's my nonna's mom, my great-grandmother," Paul said, pointing to one of the infants, "and her twin sister Carla. And these are her parents," he added, indicating an adult man and woman. Then he tapped the oldest man at the center of the photo. "And that's her own grandfather. Calogero."

Taviano's skin prickled as he gazed at the photo. It should have been difficult to recognize the young man nearing twenty-one that Taviano had last seen. Yet he would have known that face anywhere. He traced a light finger over the clear material protecting the picture. There were the almond-shaped eyes that had crinkled at the corner when Gero laughed.

"I don't understand how this is possible," he whispered. That he would find a descendant of his one-time lover in a different country on a Christmas Eve was baffling. The odds of it were smaller than the motes of dust he could track with vampire eyes. Unlikely as finding two identical snowflakes.

While Taviano lost himself in the photograph, Paul returned to the trunk. Bending over it, he rummaged some more until a series of plinks rattled the windowpane. "What was that?" he asked.

"Hmm?" Taviano murmured as he dragged his eyes from the scrapbook. He distantly registered the clattering noise but hadn't yet isolated its cause. The demon suddenly roared in his chest. Paul was already raising the sash to see who tossed stones at his apartment. He leaned over the sill.

"No, don't—!" Taviano cried out and launched himself across the room to pull him back inside the shield of the barrier magic. At the same moment, Paul yelled and thrashed as something grabbed him by the hair. His kicking feet shattered the window, raining glass down in the apartment. Taviano instinctively covered his eyes and in that instant, Paul was dragged out into the night.

The vampire with purple and blue streaks in her hair carried Paul across the gap to the rooftop beyond. She whirled to face Taviano as she forced Paul to his knees, his head yanked back to expose his neck. The sharp claws of her free hand flexed against his jugular.

Preternatural senses registered three other vampires. They arrayed themselves across the roof, near the woman who claimed the North End. The demon in Taviano's belly twisted and roared in its furious drive.

Kill maim conquer consume.

His own rage and desperation fueled the fire. It was all he

could manage to keep from leaping unprepared across the distance and tearing into the four vampires. Each was younger than him and weaker, but collectively... He didn't know if he could take on four and survive.

The woman hissed, her vicious sounds carrying easily to his ears. "I warned you but you're still here. Your familiar dies first and then we will destroy you." Her hand pulled back as she prepared to kill Paul and there was no time to think. Taviano launched himself through the shattered window, his hands stretched and fingers curled to tear out the woman's eyes.

He'd cleared the roof when one of the other vampires surged forward. It took him by surprise, grabbing an arm to pull him off balance. They crashed to the shingles together and the vampire twined around Taviano in a flash. Legs crushing Taviano's ribs, it tried to get hands at his neck.

Taviano's command slipped and his demon roared its lust and fury as it whipped his arms and legs impossibly. He somersaulted into the air and flipped so the grasping vampire was underneath him. Coming down on his back, he smashed it into the roof. The blow stunned the creature into releasing its hold.

Freed, Taviano spun to tear into the woman and time seemed to stop. Her black eyes glittered, and she smiled cruelly as she raked her nails across Paul's throat. Blood gushed out and he gave a horrible, wet cry as he tried to cover the wounds with his hands. She tossed him to the far edge of the roof.

"Paul!" Taviano wailed but even as he started to run toward his lover, the woman leapt at him. She crashed her fists against the sides of his head and he went down, groggy. Despite the ringing in his head, he could hear Paul make a ghastly whistling sound as he tried desperately to suck in air.

He fought again to break away, to get to Paul, but one of the other vampires appeared at his back. It seized him in an iron grip as the woman again made claws of her hands and swiped brutally at his face. Misery welled inside Taviano. Paul was dead or dying and it was his fault. He should have left earlier. He should never have gone to Paul's home in the first place.

The woman unleashed a series of pounding blows against his chest until he felt ribs crack. His shirt scorched under her fists. The internal damage began to repair itself but the vampire behind him put a knee against his back. It pulled on his arms as if to rip them off.

Taviano had no idea how much damage he could recover from. He didn't know if he should even try to resist. He was a monster after all. The one man who had seen him as anything better had died. Paul drew him back to Mass, made love to him, called him an angel, gave him Christmas…and he was gone.

Maybe, just maybe, if Taviano died that night too, they could meet again on the other side. He had no hope of rising to heaven. If there were a merciful God, though, perhaps He'd allow one more moment with Paul before whatever awaited him began.

Weakened, broken, hurting, he went numb as a third vampire joined the fray. It yanked Taviano's head roughly to one side, using handfuls of his hair. It bent to bite him in its own blood lust. His demon all but screamed at him to fight back, but his despair kept it trapped.

Ichor

The word whispered through his head and he had no idea where it came from. It was a voice, not a thought.

Look

And again. What was that? But a twitch drew his vampire eyes to Paul's body, sprawled on the snowy roof.

It twitched again, and Paul raised a hand to his throat. Taviano choked back a cry for fear of alerting the vampires tearing at him. Paul ran fingers over his neck as he pushed up on one elbow. Under the wet blood, the wounds had nearly healed.

How? gave way almost at once to *Of course.* Plentiful amounts of ichor spread through Paul's body from their lovemaking. It took just a trace to repair a surface wound. Taviano's drawn-out orgasm had injected far more than that, and the magic substance coursed through his organs and blood. When the woman ripped his throat open, it healed him from within.

He sent desperate thoughts at Paul, *willing* him to run while he still had a chance.

Fight

That voice. Inside him. Not in his head entirely, but through his whole body. Echoing and trying to make him stand and give battle.

It was his demon, *speaking* to him. Its rage gave voice to its passion.

Paul rolled onto his knees, then stood shakily. He wasn't running. What was he doing? Looking for a weapon.

No, Paul, don't! You won't survive another attack like that!

Give me dominion. The demon's words were clearer, echoing with its desperation. *Before it's too late, surrender to me.*

Taviano thought furiously at it, *When I gave in to you before, you killed everyone in that village. I can't let you.*

You must or it all ends. I end, you end, your familiar ends.

Taviano bellowed as the woman scored a swipe across one eye, blinding him. Already he heard bones crunching in his arms as the vampire behind him pulled. At any second the ligaments in his shoulders would give way. The one at his neck got his fangs in place and punctured the skin.

The demon raged in his head. *I promise I will spare him. Give me command and he will be safe. Before it's too late, surrender to me.*

No one but these vampires must die, Taviano pleaded with it. *Swear and I will give you my body.*

I swear.

And so Taviano surrendered.

It was as if he shrank inside his own head. He barely heard the howl of challenge and fury that ripped from his body. His demon claimed control of limbs, eyes and ears. Fangs. His bones and tendons, his eye, his neck healed instantly. The magic that he tried hard to keep contained whipped out and a wild gale threw the vampire at his neck across the roof.

His head smashed back against the one pulling at his arms, connecting with its nose. The blow stunned the creature enough that Taviano's demon broke free. Whirling, his demon grabbed the woman so quickly she never saw it coming. Her body burned in his grasp but he barely felt the pain.

Rip rend tear consume

The words pulsed around Taviano in his cocoon. His consciousness lay muffled somewhere far down inside his own body. Yet he shared the moment of triumph as his demon plunged its fangs into the woman's neck and drained all of her essence. She shrieked and twisted but was helpless in its unrestrained grasp. Taviano felt the bloodbeast that had inhabited her get sucked into his body. His demon devoured its magic and its puissance, and its awareness faded to nothing.

Then it turned on the vampire that had tried to rip off his arms and returned the favor. Ichor leapt from the man's exposed shoulder socket and swirled in the night air instead of splashing to the ground. His demon sucked in the streaming ichor, draining the vampire before his body could heal. That vampire too died as the growing mass that was his demon consumed the other bloodbeast.

And his own demon was *larger*. Even from within his nest Taviano could tell that. It took the magic of these other creatures and grew more dangerous, more powerful.

The two remaining vampires rushed away but they hadn't even crossed the roof when his demon commanded, "Stop." Thunder rolled across the shingles and rumbled loudly in the night air. There was no arguing with a voice that powerful and they must have feared they weren't fast enough to escape. Both came to a halt, quivering with their panicked need to flee, knowing they had no choice but to obey.

The demon spoke with Taviano's mouth, in words resounding with the roar of a hurricane. "I claim this territory. Leave every inhabitant of the North End unmolested and you may live. Touch as much as a rat and I will know. I will consume you as I did these hosts. Spread the word." The vampires hesitated until it shouted, "Go!"

They went.

His bloodbeast basked and glowed and preened. Its pride, its power, were glorious. It could bide its time but one night it would take to the wind again. It would consume and grow greater still.

"Taviano?"

Paul's voice drew the creature's attention. It could see him pulsing with life and blood and all the delicious things that Taviano had felt when his prick was inside. The ichor that had saved Paul's life was almost spent but traces still shone in his eyes and resonated in his voice. Paul asked, "Are you all right? Please, what's happening?"

Deep inside, so far he couldn't even tell in which direction Paul stood, Taviano heard the question. He felt his bloodbeast's hunger. *You swore*, he thought furiously at it. *He's mine. Dammit, you swore.*

He sensed his demon ponder. Its desires were alien to Taviano, its plans inchoate. Yet Taviano bore it some kinship. The thing had been inside him for nearly two centuries. Though they had never before communed in words, it had let him know its demands and its hungers.

Taviano struck out in the same way. He imagined his hands were claws tearing free of the cotton that swaddled him. He roared his passion for Paul, his loneliness, his will to protect that fragile man. His emotions throbbed against his demon's mind while he wrestled for command. He fought to tear through the cocoon and regain charge of his body.

His demon was vast, far greater than it had been before, certainly larger than Taviano's little body. Even as he railed and fought, he knew the battle was hopeless. It had grown too big, too powerful. He despaired.

But the most shocking thing happened. It turned all of its attention on Taviano and what poured back through their link felt like affection. Amusement. Maybe respect. His mind emerged from its nest and he became aware again of hands, feet, blinking eyes, a beating heart.

I keep my word, his demon told him. *I have achieved my goals for now. The rest will come in time.*

What do you mean?

You were sad. Confused. Weary. A ripple that felt like laughter. *Useless to me. So I guided you here.*

To Boston?

To a home. To this man. We have all the time there is, if we choose. You may spend some of that for yourself now.

You knew he was Calogero's descendant, didn't you? None of it was a coincidence—coming to Boston for Christmas, listening to the Mass at St. Stephen's, noticing that Paul was in trouble. More amusement from the creature, and a touch of smug pride, pulsed through their connection. *But how?*

I'm magic, it whispered.

And then Taviano controlled his own body once more. His

bloodbeast nestled and seemed to sleep in his heart and in his mind, quiet now. Satiated. Content.

Paul extended a hand tentatively and rested it on Taviano's arm. "Are you all right? I heard a voice that didn't sound like you. It made *whatever* this shit is inside me vibrate at first but I don't feel that anymore."

Taviano trembled slightly as he surveyed the rooftop and gazed out at the lights of the North End. The smell of more snow on its way tickled his nose, and the towers of Boston glistened in the distance. There was life all around him. He could hear music from some apartment close by, along with laughter and lust and joy. The desiccated remains of the two vampires were black lumps on the rooftop; he'd have to deal with those before resting.

Resting. The revelation shook him to his core. *Here. Tonight, and tomorrow, and the next night.*

Taviano drew Paul into his arms. "I'm all right. Better than that. I've claimed the North End." He heard the awe in his own voice. He could wake in the same place, evening after evening. No more endless wandering. No need to skirt the edges of a territory, hoping to pass through the world unnoticed. He scooped Paul into his arms and whirled them both around. This place was *his*.

An even stranger thought followed. *Maybe Paul could be mine too.* A demon with its own agenda brought them together, but Taviano could no longer deny his heart. He wanted to know everything about the fearless, generous man who bought presents secretly for homeless children. Who welcomed him into his home and into his body. Who gave him back the peace of the Mass and taught him he might not be a monster after all.

He slowed their spin and leaned away to watch Paul's eyes as he said softly, "I can stay here. If you still want me to."

"In Boston?" Paul asked hoarsely and his eyes glistened.

"With me?"

Cautiously, Taviano confessed, "I'd love to spend more time with you, yes. But we've only known each other for one night and it's been astonishing in every sense."

Some perversity required him to remind Paul of what he was. He tilted Paul's head back to examine his throat where the wounds had healed, leaving behind gory streaks of red. Bending, he began to lap at the blood and felt Paul inhale sharply and then purr against him like a kitten.

When Paul's neck was clean, he raised his head again and found sparkling blue eyes watching him. "I'm not exactly a catch. You may see things more clearly after you sleep. If you wake tomorrow and realize this is a mistake, believe me that I will understand and accept your choice."

Paul drew him into a fiery kiss. The passion between them seemed as powerful in its own way as his demon's magic. When he pulled back, it was to growl, "Taviano, you don't seem to get it. Your ninja stuff is awesome, sure. And I don't really under-stand the bloodbeast-vampire thing yet. But I met a kind man tonight who helped me when he could have turned away. You make me feel special and protected and wanted." He put hands on either side of Taviano's face and held his gaze. "Sure it's only been a few hours. But every great love story begins somewhere. Maybe this is ours."

The sincerity behind his eyes humbled Taviano. He didn't want to darken Paul's happiness by arguing and... Perhaps there *was* something real between them. Time would tell.

The demon throbbed amusement against his heart and made him smile. He nodded. "I'll stay as long as you want me here. Not a night more."

Paul practically attacked that time. He kissed Taviano so thoroughly that their earlier explorations seemed like mere hints of what could be. His heart beat wildly as he ground his erection against Taviano's hip. Breaking free, he said joyfully, "That's going to be a very, very long time."

Taviano answered with a smile. "Then it's a good thing I'm immortal."

NINE

TAVIANO FINALLY CONVINCED Paul to go to bed in the early hours of the morning. He promised to be back at nightfall. Then, with the few hours that left before sunrise, he disposed of the dead vampires' remains.

As he considered his nest for the day, something occurred to him. The woman he deposed must have had a lair. Testing the bond with his demon, he pulsed a question at it. Whether it gained the memories of the absorbed bloodbeasts, or through its own magic, Taviano found he knew just where to go.

He leapt easily from roof to roof, amazed and delighted at the greater strength in his limbs. Shortly, he rested on the ledge of a townhouse on North Street; a plaque in stone dated it to 1901. His demon guided him to an unlocked steel hatch set into the roof. It was so heavy it would take three or four mortals to lift. He raised it easily and crept down the staircase revealed.

Extending all of his senses, he determined that the house was empty and began to explore. Several bedrooms contained out-of-date furniture. The bathrooms' fixtures were old and rust-stained. A library's bookshelves lay empty. A living room stored furniture that may once have been luxurious but had grown shabby and worn.

In the brick-lined basement, another heavy, metal door

opened to reveal a spacious, un-windowed room. The woman had no doubt used it as her lair. A very comfortable king-size bed rested against one wall. Deep, upholstered chairs and elegant tables of gleaming wood completed the space. Something about the room spoke of a masculine, English style. That puzzled him until he abruptly knew the woman took the house for herself from the vampire she deposed.

Interesting. That suggested the place now belonged to Taviano, by right of his having claimed the North End from her.

He wandered the room, touching smooth surfaces and luxurious fabrics, and stopped before a large inlaid box. Inside were wads of cash, bits of jewelry, expensive watches and similar portable treasures. The woman had apparently been a magpie, gathering those things from her victims. A quick search revealed no stolen wallets or identification. He had nothing that could help return anything to the original owners. If they even lived, which Taviano doubted.

His demon grew restless and fretful, its way of letting him know that dawn was near. Slipping several hundred dollars and one elegant wristwatch into his pockets, he closed the box and left the lair. He would have plenty of time to explore further, and he wanted to sleep near Paul.

Paul. Even his name brought a sense of eagerness and excitement.

Closing the rooftop hatch behind him, he returned to the shabby apartment building. The storage room was right where Paul had indicated. He broke the lock, barricaded the door from inside, and made a bed for the day.

•   •   •

WHEN THE SUN set on Christmas night, Taviano opened his eyes, briefly confused by his surroundings. He lay in a dusty room.

Smells came to him, of old wood and rusting metal, and a dead rodent in the walls. The distant aroma of tomatoes and garlic was tantalizing. Where was he? But then he remembered.

He remembered his dreams too. They'd been vivid but not of his own experiences. Gradually he'd recognized even in his sleep they were a mix of memories from the two consumed blood-beasts.

By the time he awoke, he'd learned many things he needed to know. He understood how Boston worked, and knew other places where the woman had stashed spoils from her victims. He knew as well her affinity to fire was as natural to her as his was to air. That thought he filed away for further contemplation. She'd had no more need than Taviano for money but she had a taste for the blood of wealthy people, and for pretty things.

At least no more humans in the North End would die so needlessly.

Putting the deposed vampire out of his mind, Taviano focused. He realized he could hear Paul bustling around his apartment four floors above. He was singing "Good King Wenceslas" off-key but with great enthusiasm. Taviano rose from the pallet he'd made for himself and slipped out of the storage room.

He rapped at Paul's apartment for politeness, grinning with anticipation. The singing stopped and rapid footsteps crossed the floor. The door swung open and there was his Paul, with glowing eyes, unruly hair, and delighted smile.

"'Sup, bae!" he cried and launched himself at Taviano. Grabbing his head in both hands, they kissed like they hadn't seen each other for months instead of hours.

Laughing, Taviano scooped up Paul. He carried him into the apartment, reaching back with one foot to kick the door closed. He registered a blur of warm light, but only had eyes for Paul.

They ended on the futon, with Paul wriggling out of his T-shirt and jeans as Taviano also undressed.

Naked, they lay pressed together again, Taviano on his back as he stroked Paul's hair out of his eyes. "Merry Christmas," he said softly.

Paul smiled at him warmly. "You too, Taviano. I'm so glad to see you." He swiveled his hips, causing his hard cock to slide against Taviano's erection. "I think you're glad to see me too," he murmured cheekily.

"Let me show you how glad." Taviano turned their bodies until Paul's prick rested against his lips and his own brushed Paul's mouth. The taste of arousal was as delicious in its own way as blood. He didn't know which felt better—the tongue on him or the warm reality of a cock in his mouth.

He took his cues from Paul, mirroring him as Paul gently squeezed his balls and pulled him deep into his throat. When Paul stroked between his legs to brush maddeningly over his entrance, Taviano echoed it. Every way of touching was new and exquisite. Plentiful precome coated Taviano's tongue as Paul thrust his hips to get further into Taviano's mouth.

Remembering how Paul had reacted to fangs at his carotid, Taviano squeezed his erection around the base. Pulling back until a few inches remained in his mouth, he very lightly dragged his eyeteeth over the shaft. Paul gasped and stopped sucking to rest his forehead against the futon. Taviano stroked him firmly and positioned the wide shaft so it lay between his fangs. The deadly points formed a gateway to his throat.

Paul spasmed and thrust harder between the ivory spikes. He cried out and came in great splashes of semen that coated Taviano's tongue. He was still twitching when he took Taviano's cock into his mouth again; in seconds it was his turn to explode. Paul swallowed down the ichor eagerly. Taviano found to his relief he was able to control the urge to come over and over like the night before.

They lay there, nursing gently on each other's softening prick. Paul finally crawled back up Taviano's body to kiss him. The tastes of ichor and come mingled on their tongues, creating something uniquely of them.

Finally they rested with Paul's head on Taviano's shoulder. He murmured, "Dude, I don't know what's better. The way you fuck or the way you suck."

Taviano kissed his brow. "Luckily you don't have to choose. Tell me about your day?"

"My day was nowhere near as interesting as my night, believe me. Let's see. I dragged myself out of bed at six to go to the diner. Even with your magical healing juice, my ass let me know all over again that it had been well and truly fucked."

He ran his tongue up Taviano's neck to his jaw and finished by blowing a raspberry against the skin there. "And *that* meant I had to jerk off in the shower, which made me a few minutes late. After my boss reamed out my poor abused ass all over again, I started cooking for the hordes that couldn't or didn't want to be home on Christmas morning. They kept me moving until about three. Then I stopped by the shelter to help with some dinner prep."

Taviano frowned. "You mean after working all day you still had to cook more?"

"Dude! No. It's, like, a privilege to help out at the shelter. High-key *love* doing that anyway, but today was supercool. I got to hear over and over again about the intruder last night who left a shit-ton of gifts. Your trick totally worked, by the way. The youngest kid there is Cody and when he showed me his new Pokémon ball, he whispered, 'Santa brought this.'"

"I wish they knew all you did to make that happen," Taviano

said, but Paul shook his head.

"That's sweet but I don't need it. I want them to have one nice day before they go back to worrying about shit. Anyway, after I did some shopping, I came back here and went a little Christmas crazy myself. Which you totally missed because you couldn't get my dick into your mouth fast enough. And BT dubs, the thing with your fangs? Hell to the yes!"

Taviano swung them upright despite a groan of protest. "Let's see the Christmas magic then." Paul had indeed gone all out. Strands of colored lights swooped across the brick walls of the studio. A stuffed bear in a Santa hat nestled next to the little tree, and candles glowed from every free surface. Paul had set the small kitchen table with glasses of red wine and a poinsettia. Taviano realized that the aroma of tomatoes and garlic came from a pot on Paul's two-burner stove.

"I don't know if you eat people food or stuff, but I figured, just in case…" Paul blushed as he trailed off.

"That smells wonderful. And yes, I can eat and drink a little. I'd love to taste your cooking."

Paul tugged up a pair of ripped sweatpants and Taviano put his trousers on again before they sat. The pasta in a marinara sauce was tangy with a touch of sweetness. Taviano could taste the basil, oregano and black pepper Paul had used.

"This reminds me of my mama's cooking," Taviano said, clinking his glass against Paul's. "And the wine is very nice."

"My nonna gave me the bottle when I stopped by yesterday afternoon to wish her a merry Christmas."

Taviano could eat no more than a few mouthfuls because what his body had to do to purge human food was awkward. The wine was easier to handle; he sipped while Paul ate and peppered Taviano with questions.

He wanted to know more about being a vampire, about his

family, about the best places he'd wandered. Taviano got his turn, learning about a trip to Italy when Paul graduated from high school.

Once they finished dinner, Paul tugged Taviano back to the futon. "Leave the dishes. I can do them tomorrow because I'm not gonna waste a minute of our time together with something lame like that." Two packages that hadn't been there the night before had appeared under the little tree. Paul retrieved the presents and pressed them into Taviano's hands. "It isn't much, but I wanted to get you something."

Under the wrappings were a new black shirt and pants. "Thank you. These look like they'll fit perfectly."

Paul grinned. "I thought about getting red, because of the Great Santa Caper. Then I realized that wearing black is probably in the vampire code."

"Something like that," Taviano agreed with an answering smile. "It's a time-honored tradition for creatures of the night." He pulled the wristwatch out of his pants pocket. "Speaking of time," he began. "I didn't have a chance to buy you a Christmas present yet but I'd like to give you this." He fixed the band around Paul's arm.

Paul looked at the watch face with wide eyes. "This is a Piaget," he gasped, mispronouncing the name. "Holy fuck. I got you a few clothes from the discount store."

Taviano grimaced at his black shirt in the corner with its missing buttons. "I definitely needed them."

"But this watch... It's insane, Taviano. I don't know if I should take it."

"Here's the thing. It turns out that being the master of the North End, at least by vampire custom, comes with a house."

He explained about the townhouse and the treasures he'd found, then took Paul's hand. "If it bothers you about where the watch came from, I understand. But it's mine to give now. I'd like you to have a reminder of me when you're going about your day, until it's time to be together again."

Paul looked at the watch and smiled shyly. "That's a beautiful thought. Like you." He pondered for a moment. "I get it about there being no way to send it back to the original owner. Okay," he said decisively. "I'll wear it and think about you every day. Only thing is, it's awfully nice for my neighborhood. I'd kind of paint a target on my back, or my arm. Maybe I should save it to wear in the apartment?"

"About that." Taviano turned over Paul's hand to kiss his palm. "I agree about this neighborhood. I also expect I would spend most of my nights watching over you here to make sure you're safe. So I have an indecent proposition for you."

He smiled in what he hoped was a winning manner to hide his nerves. "How would you feel about living in the townhouse and helping me fix it up? It has a lot of charm but the last, uh, owner neglected it. It's probably much easier to deal with contractors and decorators in daylight hours. I have this awkward allergy to the sun…"

Saucer eyes again from Paul. "You're asking me to live with you?" he asked breathlessly.

"I suppose I am. You could leave whenever you choose, of course. And I could pay you to act as my general contractor, so you'd have your own money. You wouldn't have to keep working at the diner, unless you want to."

"Are you kidding? I love to cook but that job bites the big one." Paul grinned. "Bigger even than *your* piece, you mother-fucking sexy pile of bloodsucker." He whooped. "I'm hundo-p down with this narrative. Can you show me the house tonight?"

"Of course. It's a little dusty but we can stay there, if you like."

Paul quirked his head. "There's a safe place for you, I suppose. Can I sleep with you?"

"I've never slept near anyone human since I became a vampire. I honestly don't know if it'd be safe." That sobered Paul. Before it could bother him, Taviano added, "At least I can stay with you upstairs until dawn."

"I'll take that for now," Paul said but he smirked. "We'll see about the rest later."

"I knew you'd be stubborn about this," Taviano said ruefully. "Oh well, I'd better get used to it."

"Damn right. Hey, uh, this may be dumb of me…"

"No, please don't censor yourself. I want to know anything you think or worry about."

"Well, it sounds like you got some serious coin out of this deal. I get you had nothing to do with where it came from, and there isn't any way to restore it, like, to the families. But it might feel good to use some of it to help people. Like, karma or whatever the Catholic equivalent might be."

Taviano nodded slowly. "That's a brilliant idea."

"It is?"

"Absolutely. It will take time to understand exactly how much money there is and to convert the jewelry to cash, but you're right. It's tainted and I don't want that to affect you. Let's find good places to put, oh, half of the money to work. How does that sound?"

"It sounds fantastic!" Paul beamed. "And I know a great place to start."

"The shelter?"

"Right. Damn, they need so much help. Workers to fix the building. Paint. Better furniture and clothes for the residents—"

"Done. Consider it part of your new job, then, to get contractors lined up for the shelter as well."

Paul blinked and bit his lower lip. "I want to, but... Taviano, I'm not really qualified to manage construction or money or a philanthropy. What if I fuck this up?"

Taviano pulled him to his feet and into an embrace. "Paul, we already trust each other with our lives. You, when you make love with a vampire. Me, because you'll know where I sleep and that all it takes to destroy me is a bit of sunlight. I think we can figure out how to make the rest of it work." He kissed Paul soundly and leaned back with a smile. "Right, dude?"

Paul took a steadying breath. "'Kay 'kay. We can do this. Now will you take me to Castle Dracula? I want you to fuck me in a real bed."

Taviano growled and opened his jaw to rest his fangs against Paul's throat. He reveled in the gasp it evoked, and the shiver that ran down Paul's body. Already he felt his cock stirring, and his demon's contentment. It had exactly what it wanted: for Taviano to find passion and purpose.

Could it last? He would have to feed, and Paul might grow troubled by that. Or by the source of their wealth, or a million other details about sharing a home with a fiend. Someday soon, Paul would ask Taviano to drink from him while they made love. He'd want to know what it was like, and Taviano would have a hard time resisting.

And if they survived all that, it seemed inevitable that Paul would one day ask Taviano to turn him. At that moment, Taviano was confident he would refuse the request with every ounce of his strength. He would *not* condemn Paul to the eternal darkness that was his fate.

But Paul made his own light, and Taviano's demon had its own plans. His resolve might not be enough to deny the combined will of the man working his way into his heart and the creature that already lived there.

He shook his head clear while Paul gathered a few things he'd need. Those were problems for another time. And as his demon said, they had all the time in the world if they chose.

"Ready?" he asked, taking Paul's hand. "Let's go spend Christmas night in our new home. Together."

"You know, my nonna already thinks I'm easy. What's she gonna say when she finds out I'm shacking up with a two-hundred-year-old guy from Naples?" At Taviano's no-doubt shocked expression, Paul burst into laughter and mock-punched him in the shoulder. "JK, dude. Just kidding. Let's go find out if I'm naughty or nice." He winked. "The safe money is on naughty."

THE END

Thank you for reading *Vampire Claus*. I hope it put you in the holiday spirit!

Subscribe to my newsletter at *robertwinterauthor.com* for giveaways, my latest book news, LGBT romance recs and deals, and more! I won't spam or share your email address.

If you did enjoy the book, **please consider writing a review** on Amazon, Goodreads or other sites that discuss MM romance. I appreciate any feedback, no matter how long or short. It's a great way to let other romance fans know what you thought about this book. Being an independent author means that every review really does make a huge difference, and I'd be grateful if you take a minute to share your opinion with others.

2017 Rainbow Award honorable mention

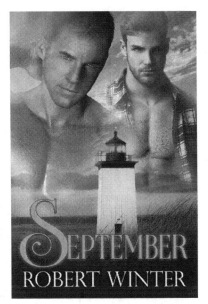

"September is a book filled with hurt and comfort, moving on and finding love, and living your best life."
—Joyfully Jay

"The emotional pull in this story is unbelievable. … The writing was captivating and the characters were remarkable."
—Love Bytes

"[Winter'] writing and storytelling ability are both beautifully brilliant, with characters that are full of emotion, and their plight and struggles real."
—Alpha Book Club

Excitement for *Lying Eyes* by Robert Winter

Five stars

"Every book gets better... This is an easy recommendation, even more so if you're a romantic mystery and/or suspense maven."
—Hearts on Fire

"Robert Winter is now an auto-buy author for me. Spectacular writing!!!"
—Amazon reviewer

"There are pulse-racing action scenes to go along with the intrigue and building romance, and an ending that goes above and beyond to supply gratification to the reader, as well as to the characters."
—It's About the Book

"4.5 stars!!"
—Bayou Book Junkies

"Robert Winter has definitely made it onto my favorite author list. This is his third book, and they just keep getting better!"
—Scattered Thoughts and Rogue Words

ABOUT THE AUTHOR

Robert Winter lives and writes in Provincetown. He is a recovering lawyer who prefers writing about hot men in love much more than drafting a legal brief. He left behind the (allegedly) glamorous world of an international law firm to sit in his home office and dream up ways to torment his characters until they realize they are perfect for each other.

When he isn't writing, Robert likes to cook Indian food and explore new restaurants. He splits his attention between Andy, his partner of sixteen years, and Ling the Adventure Cat, who likes to fly in airplanes and explore the backyard jungle as long as the temperature and humidity are just right.

Contact Robert at the following links:

Website: www.robertwinterauthor.com

Facebook: facebook.com/robert.winter.921230

Goodreads: goodreads.com/author/show/16068736.Robert_Winter

Twitter: twitter.com/@RWinterAuthor

Email: RobertWinterAuthor@comcast.net

Made in the USA
Middletown, DE
30 June 2018